# THE GREEN GANG

# THE
# GREEN GANG

## Aileen Hunter

CANONGATE · PRESS

*For Amy . . .*

First published in 1992 by Canongate Press,
14 Frederick Street, Edinburgh EH2 2HB

© 1992 by Aileen Hunter

Cover artwork by Alexa Rutherford

ISBN 0 86241 364 8

Typeset by Falcon Typographic Art Ltd,
Edinburgh
Printed and bound in Great Britain By
Cox & Wyman Ltd, Reading, Berkshire

CANONGATE PRESS PLC
14 Frederick Street, Edinburgh EH2 2HB

# 1

'Give me the binoculars! Quickly Donna!'

'What is it?' asked Jimbo, straining to see what Robbie was pointing at.

'It's one of the buzzards, the male I think.'

'Wow! I think I see it,' whispered Donna, trying to block out the sun with her hands. 'It's over by that wee hump.'

'That's just a clod of mud,' argued Jimbo, 'it's far too still for a bird.'

'It's a bird all right,' croaked Robbie excitedly, and it's one of the buzzards. It's got a head like a golden eagle, but its lower legs don't have any feathers, it's the right colour – a sort of chocolate brown – have a look Jimbo.'

'But why is it so still?' asked Donna. 'Is it asleep, or dead?'

'No, it must be waiting by a mouse's hole or something. They can stay there for hours, not moving an inch, just to catch a mouse.'

'Well, good on it,' mused Donna. 'I wish there was a buzzard for every mouse.'

'There aren't that many,' advised Robbie.

Their bird-watching expedition had indeed proved fruitful. Robbie had promised them something special and there it was – a bird of prey.

'Are they really rare?' asked Donna, nudging Jimbo to give her the binoculars. 'Come on, you've had long enough.'

They started to struggle with each other.

'Stop it!' hissed Robbie. 'You'll scare it away! They are not extinct, but like all birds of prey they are protected. You're not allowed to bother them.'

Donna put the glasses to her eyes and everything was a blur.

'You've mucked up that focus on purpose haven't you,' she accused Jimbo.

She fiddled about with the lenses.

'You're a bam-pot Jimbo!'

'Ssshhh,' hissed Robbie. 'Here, let me fix them for you.'

'I've got it, I've got it!' rasped Donna. 'Wow it's a corker!'

'They nest in the trees up there,' said Robbie, pointing at a wooded area a few hundred metres away from the spot where the bird now sat. 'They make nests of twigs and line them with moss and leaves and sometimes hair.'

'Human hair?' asked Jimbo.

'Hardly,' sneered Donna. 'How many buzzards have you seen swooping down and pinching someone's hair?'

'I was only asking,' Jimbo pointed out, turning away in an effort to hide his red face. 'Is it still there?'

Donna peered through the binoculars once more.

'I've lost it – it's gone,' she wailed.

'Typical,' complained Jimbo. 'Typical female –

too much talking and not enough paying attention.'

'There it is,' yelled Robbie, taking no notice of
his friends quibbling. 'Give me the glasses!'

He rushed them to his eyes and pointed them
high into the sky.

'He's got it! He's got the mouse. He'll be taking
it back to the nest!'

'Hope his wife's got the chips on,' laughed Jimbo.
'There's nothing like a plate of good old mice and
chips and a pickled onion.'

'Delicately washed down with some Irn Bru,'
joked Robbie.

'Yeuch,' said Donna screwing up her face.

'What's wrong?' asked Robbie. 'Don't you like
Iron Bru?'

'Ha ha,' said Donna as she picked herself up
off the grass and brushed bits of straw from her
clothes.

'We'll have to come back to see the buzzard again,'
said Jimbo, tying the lace of his desert boot.

'As long as we're careful, it should be all right. I
wonder if they've laid their eggs yet. April is their
breeding time,' Robbie informed them.

'Can you tell a buzzard by the noise it makes?'
asked Donna.

'It goes . . . sort of . . . peee-oooo!' replied Robbie.

'That's not very exciting is it – peee-oooo,' said
Jimbo.

'It's not bad,' said Robbie. 'I saw a programme
on the telly recently where a man taped the sound
of a nightingale singing, then slowed it down until he

9

could copy it and he was convinced that it sounded just like the music Beethoven composed.'

'What did he write?' asked Jimbo.

'Classical stuff,' replied Robbie.

'Well, I can't see a conductor leading a chorus of peee-ooo – can you?'

'You're never going to be musical are you Jimbo?' mused Donna.

'No, Robbie's the one who blows his own trumpet. I just fix things.'

'Come on then Jim'll fix it. Let's go home and you can put the chain back on my bike.'

'Are you coming over to the farm tonight?' Robbie asked her. 'We're really going to sicken Ally and watch the video of Scotland winning the rugby Grand Slam again.'

'Plus we've got a corker of a video,' said Jimbo excitedly. 'Cretins!'

'Critters, you bam-pot,' corrected Robbie. 'It's about a load of furry round things that eat everyone in sight.'

'Sounds tasty,' said Donna grinning, 'but I'm going swimming with Shanghita and Karen tonight.'

Her expression changed to a sad one. She felt a bit out of things with the girls these days.

'Just be sure there are no Cretins lurking in the depths of the pool then,' warned Robbie, seeing her expression and nudging her encouragingly.

'Ally and Jimbo will be with you so we should be safe enough,' said Donna with a rueful grin.

They wandered back towards the town along the River Tweed whose banks were aglow with daffodils. The river valley was surrounded by hills. Some were dotted with sheep right up to the summit and others were thick with forestry. Near the summit of the highest hill, there was still a little pocket of snow which had remained since the last of the blizzards in February. It would move when the sun got higher, but for now there was still a shadow cast over it keeping the temperature at that height too low to bring a thaw.

'It's Easter Sunday tomorrow,' pointed out Jimbo. 'Will we go and roll our eggs as usual?'

'Perhaps I'll find the one I lost last year,' said Robbie. 'It was a piece of art too.'

'It would be,' mused Jimbo. 'It would be . . .'

# 2

The public swimming baths in Tweedvale had recently been modernised and they sat high on one of the hills looking down over the picturesque town. The building also housed two games halls, a gymnasium and a snack bar, thus it was always buzzing with people of all ages and interests. The local rugby teams trained in the gymnasium twice a week and then used the pool. Therefore, girls were not allowed to use the pool on Tuesdays and Thursdays. They were quite happy to keep out of the way on those nights anyway. Who wanted to be confronted by a crowd of big smelly men and boys?

Every other evening the girls could use the pool as they pleased and on this particular Saturday evening they were not surprised to find the building quieter than usual. After all, the school children had been on holiday for almost a fortnight and many of them had had enough of swimming for a while.

Both Karen and Shanghita were sporting new swimming costumes and Donna felt rather dowdy in her old costume which she was having to squeeze into nowadays. Her friends did nothing to reassure her. Sometimes Donna got the impression, especially from Karen, that she wasn't really welcome. Financially, Donna could not compete with the girls and that seemed to make her the odd one out.

'You should have come to Edinburgh shopping with us,' Karen told her. 'We bought lots and lots of summer clothes.'

'Mum says I might get a few things at the end of the month,' said Donna. 'Perhaps the two of you could come with us then.'

'Yes,' enthused Shanghita. 'I love shopping.'

'We'll see,' said Karen, less certain.

Karen's mum had taken them to Pizzaland for lunch. There was no chance of Donna's mum doing that. She was mean. The last time she had taken them out was to the cinema and they were given the choice of ice cream or sweets, not both. Everyone had ice cream *and* sweets when they went to the cinema.

'What did you do this afternoon then?' Shanghita asked Donna.

'I went bird-watching with Robbie and Jimbo. We actually saw a bird of prey – a buzzard!'

'Sounds fun,' commented Karen, nudging Shanghita slyly.

'It was,' agreed Donna. 'They are pretty rare you know, and protected. Robbie knows all about them.'

'Is there ever anything Robbie doesn't know about?' asked Karen.

'He doesn't know how to stop wheezing,' giggled Shanghita.

'That isn't very fair,' said Donna. 'How would you like to have asthma?'

'I suppose,' conceded Shanghita. 'He can't help it if he's too weak to play rugby.'

13

'He can play rugby fine,' argued Donna. 'It just seems to make his asthma worse that's all.'

'Come off it Donna,' said Karen screwing her face up. 'It's just a good excuse to get out of playing. He's a big wimp! How many *real* men play the harp and the flute? Ally and Jimbo aren't much but at least they aren't pansies.'

'You really make me sick sometimes Karen,' hissed Donna. 'You're always slagging all of them off for something or other. Even darling Ally.'

'Ally's okay,' argued Karen. 'At least his dad isn't the town joke, not like Jimbo's dad.'

'Jimbo can't help having a stupid dad,' pointed out Donna.

'And Robbie can't help being a wimp,' retorted Karen. 'Let's face it Donna, they're all just little boys. We'll be going to the High School soon – then we'll see some real hunks. Not just some snotty nosed kids. I don't know why you persist in mucking about with them.'

'We've been friends for years,' argued Donna. 'We *all* have – you like them don't you?' she said to Shanghita.

Shanghita lowered her eyelids and bit her lips. 'Well . . . they are a bit juvenile aren't they?'

'I take it you two won't be coming up the hill to roll your eggs tomorrow then?'

Karen burst into peels of laughter and Shanghita grinned sheepishly.

'You must be joking,' giggled Karen. 'I think we're past *that* stage.'

'What are you going to do then? Walk up and

14

down the High Street and bat your eyelids? Or is mummy taking you somewhere expensive?'

'She might be,' said Karen. 'And you'll be missing out because you'll be busy painting faces on boiled eggs.'

'Suits me fine,' retorted Donna. 'I don't think I can get my nose high enough up in the air to go out with your mother anyway.'

'Are you calling my mum a snob?' rasped Karen.

'Like mother like daughter,' said Donna airily.

'Right that's it!' snapped Karen. 'Come on Shanghita, let's go.' She pulled herself up out of the pool. 'And you Donna can get lost. You'll just have to go out with your own mean mum from now on because we're not speaking to you. Right?'

'Fair enough,' said Donna.

'And don't bother coming into the changing room until we're gone. You'll pollute the air.'

'Okay,' said Donna. 'Anything else?'

'And . . . and . . .' said Karen thinking hard, 'and . . . you just keep out of our hair you . . . you . . . cow-bag!'

'I wouldn't wish your hair on a buzzard's nest,' whispered Donna to herself as they walked away. She fought back the tears. Crying was no good. She was better off without them anyway.

She shook herself and swam a couple of breadths of the pool. Karen was impossible. She ruled the roost and Shanghita always backed her up. They had argued before, and Donna had always given in. But not this time. She wasn't going to give Karen the satisfaction. If anyone was going to come around this time it would have to be her.

She swam around on her own for another ten minutes and then reluctantly she pulled herself up out of the water and crept into the changing rooms. They were quiet. No-one was about. Quickly, Donna dried herself and got dressed. She raked about in her bag praying that she had ten pence to phone her mum to come and collect her. Donna wasn't allowed to walk home by herself and she didn't fancy another row that night. She waited inside the entrance for her mum to arrive and prayed that Karen and Shanghita were not in the snack bar. She couldn't face them again tonight. Monday at school would be soon enough. By that time, she hoped, it would all be forgotten.

To her relief, her mum's rickety old car drew up and she dashed outside to meet her.

'What happened to the others?' she asked Donna.

'They . . . they left early.'

'Do you want some chips?'

'No thanks Mum,' replied Donna.

'I can afford a bag of chips you know,' said her mum softly.

'It's not that,' said Donna, 'I'm just not very hungry.'

'Perhaps your Dad will come with an egg for you tomorrow,' said her mum kindly.

'He forgot my birthday last month. Why should he remember an egg?'

'He's a busy man Donna,' said her mum. 'But he still loves you.'

'Humph.' Donna turned her head away towards the window only to catch sight of Karen and Shanghita standing on the corner with some first year boys who were waving their fists and sneering at her.

# 3

Donna was in no hurry to reach school on Monday morning.

She had delayed going up the hill to roll the eggs as long as she could on Sunday, hoping that her dad would appear, but eventually, they had to go and when they got back there was still no sign of him. Her mum had driven them up the hill and then the egg rolling had turned more into a race between her and Jimbo. All they had succeeded in doing was smashing the eggs to smithereens – and that was just what Donna had felt like doing – she was hurt by the non-appearance of her dad. It wasn't fair.

If Robbie was upset at them smashing his works of art, he didn't show it. He was really nice to Donna all day. Robbie was like that. He always seemed to sense when she was particularly unhappy.

Jimbo just liked to play and race and smash things. Donna liked that too. She always knew where she was with Jimbo.

When they had come back down the hill, Donna's mum had taken them for chocolate milk shakes at the Italian Café. Donna tried to enjoy herself. She knew that her mum was trying hard to make up for the disappointment Donna felt about her dad.

Donna did feel more cheerful when they went home. It had been a great afternoon. Her good mood didn't last long though. She suddenly remembered that she had to go back to school the next day.

As the evening wore on and there was no word from Karen, she began to worry more about what was in store for her at school. She had been sure that Karen would phone and everything would be sorted out – but no such luck – Donna went to bed with a great weight on her shoulders.

In the morning, she had opened a letter addressed to her and found a hastily scribbled note from her dad enclosing five pounds. Donna had tried to give it to her mum, knowing that she could do with the money for the housekeeping, but her mum had insisted that she keep it and spend it on herself. Reluctantly, Donna put the money away in her bankie. Not long ago she would have been thrilled to have been given five pounds, but not now. Money couldn't make things better now.

So here she was walking slowly towards school, dreading the thought that Karen and Shanghita were really not speaking to her. Her worst fears were realised when she walked into the classroom. All of the girls stared straight at her but none of them spoke. She sat down in the only available desk a bank of two at the very front – but since everyone, else was in she knew that she would be sitting alone. Karen and Shanghita sat directly behind her.

'Have you noticed that smell?' asked Karen in a voice just loud enough for Donna to hear.

Donna wanted to turn round and say something

but she already wanted to cry and she was afraid of what else Karen might have to say.

'It's like rotten eggs,' continued Karen, 'someone must have been rolling in them – probably couldn't afford the electricity to boil them first.'

'Who rolls eggs nowadays anyway?' asked Shanghita.

'Just the pathetic little girls who can't afford a chocolate one,' sneered Karen.

Donna wanted to turn round and tell them that she had enough money to buy loads of eggs. She wanted to tell them what a lovely afternoon they had had. She wanted to boast about the chocolate milk shakes. She wanted to . . . but there was no way she was going to. That would be playing right into their hands.

Donna was relieved when the class started and she tried hard to forget everything and concentrate on fractions. Arithmetic wasn't her best subject. She preferred English by far. She had a talent for writing . . . little surprise since her father was a journalist and her mother was an English teacher. At the moment she liked writing poetry. It was so interesting, trying to tell a story but having to rhyme words as well. She had been given the top mark in the school for her poem about Easter before the holidays. But for now, she was concentrating on common denominators. As the bell want for play-time, Mrs McKay's announcement shook Donna.

'Will the following people stay behind please – Karen, Donna, Shanghita, James, Robert and Alastair. The rest of you may go.'

Donna sat still. She could almost feel Karen's eyes piercing into the back of her head. Cold, hard and unfeeling. Donna shivered a little.

'What are you sitting here for Donna?' asked Jimbo as he slumped into the chair beside her. 'Thought you used to sit up the back with Karen and Shanghita.'

Donna could sense Karen's amusement at Jimbo's innocent question.

'Not now,' she mumbled.

'What do you think old Mrs Mack wants then?'

Donna shrugged her shoulders.

'What do you think?' he turned round to Karen.

'Beats me,' replied Karen. 'You and I have hardly got anything in common, have we?'

'Meeaaw,' said Robbie as he and Ally came over to lean on Donna's desk.

Donna grinned for the first time all day. Suddenly she felt safer, more protected, less vulnerable. Even if all of the girls were not speaking to her she still had the boys.

'Right then,' said Mrs McKay, breezing back into the room. 'The head master wants us to enter for a national competition. The project will be to produce an original piece – in documentary form – on the wide ranging topic of conservation. The nature of the project must be entirely decided by yourselves and you will have full responsibility for the content of it. All of the school equipment will be at your disposal, including the new video camera, and transport can be arranged if you have to go further afield than Tweedvale. The six of you have been chosen because of the variety of your talents, but you can feel free to call on the help of other classmates if you so desire. You will be given some class time for this project, but I would expect you to devote a reasonable amount of your own time to it. Is that understood?'

'Why have you chosen us?' asked Karen. 'I don't get it?'

'Karen, you are Top Girl, Shanghita has a gift for music as has Robert, who is also an expert on wildlife – the group may find this useful. Donna, of course, has a great writing talent – you will need some sort of script. Alastair is a camera buff . . .'

'And Jim'll fix it,' mused Karen. 'Looks like we're stuck with them then,' she mumbled to Shanghita.

'Right, you'd better go and have the rest of playtime. I suggest you have a preliminary meeting tonight. Once you have come up with the main ideas we can get together and discuss their feasibility.'

'As long as I don't miss "*Home and Away*,"' warned Karen.

'Ever heard of a VCR?' mumbled Jimbo.

# 4

'We've got to find a way to get Donna off this project,' urged Karen. 'I couldn't stand working with her – she'd drive me mad.'

'Yes, it will be a bit uncomfortable since we are not speaking,' mused Shanghita.

'Uncomfortable? It'll be unbearable!'

'Are you sure?' asked Shanghita.

'Look, we can handle the stupid boys all right. They'll do what they are told – eventually. But Donna will just spoil it. She'll be awkward on purpose and get right up our noses – especially if she thinks she's going to write the script.'

'She *is* good at writing though,' admitted Shanghita.

'She writes one lousy poem that gets into the local paper and a few sooky essays and suddenly she is Tweedvale's equivalent to Roald Dahl. We can manage fine without her.'

'But how are we going to put her off?' asked Shanghita.

'Simple. We'll make her so scared of us that she won't even stay back for the meeting after school. By the time we've finished with her this afternoon she'll be off home to poor old mummy like a shot. Now c'mon, let's have some lunch.'

\*    \*    \*

'What's up with Karen and Shanghita?' asked Robbie.

'They're not speaking to me,' said Donna sadly. 'We had a bit of a row on Saturday night and they've turned all the girls against me.'

'Women,' mused Jimbo, 'typical women.'

'Och, it'll all blow over in a couple of days,' said Robbie.

'Somehow I don't think it will this time,' said Donna philosophically. 'It seems much more serious – I can't say I'm looking forward to the project either. The atmosphere will be horrible if this morning is anything to go by.'

'But they'll *have* to talk to you at the meeting, won't they?' encouraged Jimbo.

'I suppose so.'

'Well then.'

'Where's Ally?' asked Robbie.

'He's run off to the High School to give one of his football mates a copy of the City video.'

'Is he still keen for you all to join the City Strollers?' asked Donna.

'He never shuts up about them,' remarked Robbie. 'The Tweedvale Casuals – the town's answer to the Mafia and he wants us to go about with them. The bam-pot worships them.'

'He *is* keen on football though,' reasoned Donna.

'So he is,' agreed Jimbo, 'but that shower don't care about the football. All they are interested in is whose head they can kick in after the match. Some of them notch up their conquests on the local bus shelters.'

'And if they're not doing that, they are terrorising

old ladies on the street,' continued Robbie. 'Ally's got a screw loose if he wants to get in tow with that crowd of loonies. He never used to care about fighting or bullying. Now most of the younger boys are scared to go near him.'

'Boys,' said Donna, shaking her head and getting her own back on Jimbo, 'typical boys.'

'Ha ha,' retorted Jimbo. 'At least boys settle their arguments instead of ignoring each other.'

'That's not really fair Jimbo,' said Robbie. 'I'm sure that Donna would sort things out with the gruesome twosome if she could.'

Donna nodded her head sadly.

'Here comes Ally now,' said Jimbo pointing to a red-faced boy who was running towards them. 'I wonder if his tongue's sore from all the boot licking he's just done. Hey Ally!'

'I thought I was going to be late,' he gasped. 'I was talking with the gang for ages and I didn't realise the time.'

'I wouldn't have thought that Strollers would worry about a silly little thing like being late,' said Robbie, grinning.

'Och away and boil your head,' retorted Ally.

'Why are you so keen on these guys anyway?' asked Donna.

'Look! We'll be going up to the High School in the Summer. We'll just be little minions to these boys. It's *safer* to join them. I don't want to get battered stupid, thank you.'

'They won't touch us,' said Jimbo, 'or they'd have the rugby team to reckon with.'

'But I don't play rugby,' argued Ally.

'Then why don't you start?' suggested Donna. 'The Strollers are just a bunch of hooligans. You'll end up in trouble.'

'It's not like that,' said Ally. 'They don't look for trouble you know, not really – and you get a good laugh with them . . . and hear good jokes and things.'

'You're wasting your time Donna,' mused Robbie. 'The sun shines out of their bottoms as far as Ally's concerned. Anyway, let's go, or we'll really be late.'

'Didn't think you rugby boys bothered about that sort of thing,' said Ally, grinning.

With that they all raced back to the classroom.

Donna had a very trying afternoon.

Firstly, every girl who passed her desk knocked something to the floor and then every time she crouched down and fished about to pick it up, Karen pulled her chair back and she almost fell when she tried to sit down again. Every so often, the point of a compass would be jabbed into her bottom, and she couldn't concentrate as she waited for the next one, so much so that she didn't hear the teacher talking to her and she got a lecture for not paying attention. Even when she tried to sit back and present a smaller target to Karen's compass, her hair was pulled with such ferocity that she was sure she would end up bald.

At afternoon play-time, she dashed to the safety of the lavatory, only to be jeered at from outside the cubicle by all the girls. She didn't try to get out, figuring that she was better off with just verbal abuse.

'Sticks and stones will break my bones . . .' she said to herself. But it was difficult to ignore their horrible comments.

When the bell went again, she stayed where she was until they had all gone and then dashed up to the classroom a little late, resulting in yet another lecture from Mrs McKay. Her relief when the finishing bell went was short lived. She stood up to go and then suddenly remembered about the project meeting. She considered going anyway, but decided against it. She was not going to give in to Karen that easily. Instead she walked over to where the boys sat and joined in with them as they kidded Ally about the football.

'Hmm Hmm!'

They carried on talking.

'*Hmm Hmm!*'

The four looked round to find Karen at the front of the classroom with her hands on her waist.

'Are we going to get started or what?' she asked, insistently.

They all looked at each other and shrugged their shoulders.

'Okay,' said Jimbo, 'C'mon up here then.'

'No,' said Karen firmly. 'You lot can come down here. I'm in charge.'

'Who says?' asked Robbie.

'Of course I am,' replied Karen. 'That's *obviously* why I was picked for this.'

'It wasn't because you had a particular talent then?' asked Robbie.

'No . . . er . . . yes . . . don't be stupid. I *am* Top Girl you know.'

'We know,' sighed Jimbo. 'But that doesn't make you in charge of this project.'

'Ha ha ha,' said Karen sarcastically. 'Who else is going to do it? None of you could run a Sunday School picnic.'

'Donna would be the obvious choice,' said Jimbo seriously.

Donna kicked him hard on the leg.

'What?' asked Karen incredulously. 'Her?'

'She *will* be writing the script,' argued Jimbo.

'Who says?' challenged Karen. 'This is going to be a joint effort.'

'In that case, we don't need someone to be in charge,' said Robbie quickly.

'I give up,' said Karen, shaking her head. 'I can see this is going to be a complete waste of time.'

'You can back out if you want,' offered Robbie. 'Mrs Mack did stress that it wasn't compulsory.'

Donna was enjoying this. Karen had bulldozed her way right into a corner. She could see her squirm.

'Why don't we all go home and have a think about it and discuss it again tomorrow before school,' suggested Shanghita, coming to her friend's rescue.

'Good idea,' agreed Karen, making for the door. 'See you tomorrow folks.' She dashed out of the door too quickly to see Donna shake Robbie's hand. It had been worth a few jabs and tugs earlier on just to have seen Karen's face as she made for a fast exit.

'I know what we'll do,' said Karen as they tore off down the school brae. 'We'll jolly well let her be in charge and then see how *she* likes being messed about. We'll make her so miserable that she'll *have* to come off the project.'

'Okay,' said Shanghita heavily. 'Can we give up the compass jabbing though – I'm not really keen on doing that.'

'Of course.' said Karen, 'Do you really think that she'll still be sitting in front of us tomorrow? Even *she* isn't that big a mug.'

# 5

Karen's new tactic hadn't worked either. Donna steadfastly refused to entertain being leader of the project and Jimbo, Robbie and even Ally had backed her to the hilt. Therefore it was decided that they would each have their own area of responsibility and could enlist any help they might require.

Donna was happy to have been left to the script writing. She already had some ideas but she had not yet had the courage to put them to the whole group – or rather to Karen. Rather than just a droning voice telling the facts, she thought that if they made a video and then used only verse and music to accompany it, the message they were trying to convey would perhaps be stronger.

She knew Karen would hate that idea. She hadn't spared Donna's feelings with her opinion of her Easter poem – and that was when she *was* speaking to her. So Donna decided to put the idea to Robbie first. He and Shanghita were collaborating on the musical aspect of the video. Although Robbie could play lots of instruments, even he would agree that Shanghita was the most talented musically. Robbie liked to make up music and fiddle about with instruments – he would make a great arranger one day, but Shanghita – she could be a concert pianist. Karen's task was to get in touch with local conservation groups and to research the subject relevant to the local area.

Donna wanted to concentrate on the beauty of the Scottish borders and its wildlife and look at ways to conserve the area. She wanted to mesmerise the judges with the contrasting hills and valleys and the sparkling waters of the River Tweed and its tributaries. She hadn't said much of this to the others yet. All Karen had harped on about so far was the fact that her father's employees' company cars had all been converted to use lead-free petrol. Very commendable too – but how were they supposed to film that?

The filming was Ally's job. His dad was a photographer and had a camera shop in Edinburgh. He commuted the thirty miles to and from the city every day. He was not alone. Tweedvale was a lovely place to live, much more peaceful than the city and the house prices were much lower than those in Edinburgh. However, the more desirable the Tweedvale properties were becoming, the more expensive they were, and the local people on rural wages were finding it increasingly difficult to afford to buy a home.

Luckily, Donna's parents had bought their home many years ago and even though her mother and father had now separated, they did still have a lovely home despite the tight budget mother and daughter now survived on. Others were not so lucky, and that was why incomers to the town were treated with a certain amount of suspicion and resentment.

On Saturday Karen and Shanghita were going to be busy shopping again but Donna and the three boys were going to go along the river, weather permitting, to take some pictures of the local countryside. Robbie had said that they might even see the buzzard again. Donna was really looking forward to it.

# 6

'We should have realised that Mrs Mack wouldn't let us have the video camera out for the weekend, not without supervision anyhow,' mused Donna.

'It's a perfect day for filming too,' said Robbie. 'Your idea about filming the beauty of things sounds good to me.'

'Do you think the others will agree?' she asked.

'I don't see why not. We have to have something concrete to put to Mrs Mack on Monday afternoon anyhow.'

'Have you discussed the music with Shanghita yet?' asked Donna.

'A bit,' replied Robbie. 'But I can't get talking with her for two minutes without Karen sticking her oar in.'

'She's going to hate the idea of doing the script in verse too,' said Donna ruefully.

'Let's face it Donna. Nothing we can do will really please her – we'll just have to out-vote her on everything.'

'Only if she's wrong though,' warned Donna. 'I'm not falling into the trap of disagreeing with her for disagreeing's sake.'

'Fair enough,' conceded Robbie, 'but how often do you think that we *will* agree with her?'

'About as often as Jimbo and Ally ever meet us on time. They are ten minutes late already.'

As it happened, the wait was worth it because Ally appeared soon after, proudly carrying his dad's video camera and Jimbo had a huge pair of binoculars around his neck, shop rejects no doubt, which seemed to be so heavy that his knees were almost skimming the ground. 'Are you sure this isn't a two-eyed telescope Ally?' he complained collapsing to the ground. 'We're not doing a project on outer space you know.'

Robbie, who was much bigger, removed the burden from Jimbo, gave him his own small glasses to carry, and happily the four strode along the river bank in search of beautiful scenery.

'You'll never believe this,' said Robbie as he looked around for inspiration. 'Dad's gone and arranged a junior rugby sevens tournament for Saturday 12th May.'

'Great,' enthused Jimbo.

'It's the same day as the Scottish Cup final,' Ally pointed out.

'Oh no,' wailed Jimbo. 'Dad's been insisting that I go to Hampden with him because City are in the final.'

'Well, you've got a good excuse now,' said Donna.

'Dad doesn't look on rugby as a good excuse to miss football,' moaned Jimbo. 'We'll have a big row now. I even said I would go to the football just to shut him up. Now he'll go crackers.'

Jimbo's dad was football crazy – he lived for the game – his only passion in life, much to his wife's

34

disgust. He had never been much of a player, but he was a self-appointed expert on the game – the only game in the world worthy of his support – 'the working man's game' as he called it. Jimbo shared his dad's enthusiasm and passion, but for rugby and he dearly wished his father would let him play if he wanted.

'It's stupid,' said Robbie. 'I want to get out of the rugby and you have the perfect excuse but want to play.'

'You hate football, Robbie,' said Ally, confused.

'I know,' admitted Robbie. 'But I thought I was finished with rugby for months. My asthma's been getting worse and worse all season. I hate getting an attack on the pitch.'

'You're a great flanker though,' encouraged Jimbo.

'But you don't know what it's like having asthma. It spoils everything. Dad just doesn't understand.'

Robbie's dad had played flanker for the South of Scotland. Two of his uncles had actually played for their country and for the British Lions. Robbie's dad had been injured just as he was on the fringe of international honours himself and had been forced to give the game up. Now, he seemed to have pinned all of his international hopes on to his only son. The burden weighed heavily on Robbie's shoulders.

'Don't worry about it yet boys,' said Donna trying to cheer them up. 'It's weeks away.'

'Well, I know what I'll be doing anyway,' said Ally. 'Come on the blues!' he sang waving an imaginary scarf in the air.

Everyone groaned.

'Where are we going anyhow?' asked Donna. 'We just seem to be wandering aimlessly.'

'Let's go and see if we can find the buzzard first,' suggested Jimbo.

'That won't be easy to film,' warned Ally.

'I'm not sure we are allowed to film birds of prey anyhow,' said Robbie.

'Surely it would be okay if we weren't bothering it,' reasoned Donna.

'Probably,' conceded Robbie. 'We shouldn't go near its nest though.'

'If you think I've got any intention of climbing a huge big tree with my dad's camera you can forget it,' said Ally with ferocity.

They sat down on the grass where they had been watching the buzzard from before and shared two cans of Irn Bru which Donna had brought along. She was pleased that for once, she was providing the snacks for their little outings. Robbie's mother usually obliged with mountains of home-made baking and lemonade, but this time it was her treat, thanks to the belated generosity of her dad.

'I can't see any birds at all,' moaned Ally. 'Can't we just take some landscape shots instead? It's a good spot – there are very few shadows and it's nice and bright.'

'Okay then,' said Robbie. 'You carry on and I'll keep a look out with the binoculars.'

'Here, you can have these,' said Jimbo, handing the smaller glasses to Donna. 'I'll keep Ally company.'

Donna found a sunny spot and knelt down again.

She looked around the countryside. It was beautiful. Many of the trees were still bare, but they contrasted starkly with the blossom already aglow and colourful on some of the others. The field in the distance was dotted with sheep and lambs. Ally would have to include them in his filming. They bounded about happily with the sun on their backs. What an idyllic early life they had.

Donna decided that she couldn't work on a farm. She would get far too attached to all of the beasts. It made her sick to imagine that many of the happy, carefree little creatures would soon wind up on a plate with mint sauce. Thank goodness they didn't know about it. They just took every day as it came. Donna prayed that they were all girls – far more of them survived than boys because the boys couldn't increase the flock the next year.

Coming out of her daydream, Donna found that she was now walking towards the field. Her foot brushed against something odd. It wasn't hard, but it was a weird feeling that automatically made her look down.

'Oh no!' she screamed. 'Robbie come here quickly! Boys help!'

Ally arrived on the scene first.

'Look,' said Donna tearfully pointing to the ground.

'It's only a dead bird Donna and half a rabbit. I thought you had seen a ghost,' he grumbled.

'It looks like . . . it looks like . . .' puffed Jimbo.

'The buzzard,' said Donna. 'Robbie will know. Robbie! Quickly!'

Robbie had been hundreds of metres away and he was struggling across the heavy ground carrying the great big binoculars. With the effort he was already feeling wheezy.

'Do you think it's been shot?' asked Ally.

'It's been poisoned,' wheezed Robbie as he bent down and put his hands on his knees. 'The rabbit . . . must have been bait.'

'Bait?' asked Jimbo.

'Poisonous bait to catch . . . I don't know . . . vermin of some kind. Buzzards are carrions. They sometimes feed on dead carcasses.'

'But so do lots of animals. Dad's dog sometimes sniffs out dead rabbits and things,' said Ally.

'Exactly. That's why baiting is illegal. I'll have to phone the R.S.P.B.'

'What's that?' asked Ally.

'The Royal Society for the Prevention of Birds,' said Jimbo smartly.

'Protection, bam-pot,' said Donna, shaking her head. 'The Royal Society for The Protection of Birds.'

'They'll have to be told right away,' gasped Robbie.

'Whose land is this?' asked Donna.

'The Reids',' said Robbie. 'The next farm to ours.'

'Oh oh,' said Ally. 'It's Bruiser Reid who's got my City video. Bruiser Reid who's big in the Strollers. Bruiser Reid who's just plain big!'

'What's that got to do with it?' asked Jimbo.

'Do you think they'll get into trouble?' Ally ventured.

'I hope so – that's downright dangerous.'

'Well, Bruiser had better not find out that I had anything to do with this. He'll murder me.'

'Don't be daft,' said Robbie. 'Now listen. I'll go home right away and phone the R.S.P.B. and the police. You lot stay here. Ally, take as much film as you can of this.'

'But what if somebody comes?' he said edgily.

'Then run away . . . but they'll need proof, so take the rabbit with you, we'll have film of the bird.'

'Won't film of the rabbit do?' asked Donna, not keen on uplifting half a rabbit.

'They'll have to test it for poison. So *remember*, don't touch it with your bare hands.'

'How can we take it away then?' asked Jimbo.

Donna emptied the crisps out of her supermarket bag. 'We can use this.'

'You probably won't have to. The police'll be here as soon as I can get to the phone,' said Robbie. 'Here, take these,' he said, handing Ally's big binoculars back to Jimbo. 'I'll be as quick as I can.'

'Can't Jimbo go?' asked Donna. 'He's a faster runner – and what about your asthma?'

'The telephone number's in my bedroom some-where,' said Robbie shrugging his shoulders. 'It'll have to be me.'

'Take care then,' said Donna, waving him off.

'I don't like this,' said a worried Ally shaking his head and looking round about him nervously. 'I don't like this at all.'

# 7

'Look Ally, just get a grip.'

'That's easy for you to say Donna – you're a female. Bruiser and his mates are hardly likely to batter you,' moaned Ally.

'I can't be sure of that,' argued Donna. 'But this . . .' she said pointing at the dead bird, '. . . this is awful. This isn't conservation . . . it's . . . it's . . .'

'It's illegal,' finished Jimbo, 'and it's what we should be basing our project on.'

'The needless slaughter of a bird of prey,' said Donna.

'Okay, okay, I'm just scared, that's all,' mumbled Ally.

'I know,' said Donna sympathetically. 'Let's concentrate on filming then.'

'There's not much to film is there,' Ally pointed out.

'Then we'll have to make it dramatic,' enthused Donna.

'Start as far away as you can and then zoom in. Once you are as close as you can get . . . em . . . run round and round in a circle keeping filming. That should be really effective.'

'It'll be a bit bumpy,' warned Jimbo.

'That shouldn't matter,' said Ally. 'The effect will be good.'

'You'd better do it a few times, just to be on the safe side – we can always edit out the bad bits,' said Jimbo.

'You keep a look out then Donna,' urged Ally. 'One sign of anyone and I'm offski.'

Ally zoomed in on the bird and rabbit from lots of different angles and then did as Donna suggested and ran round. Luckily, although the carcasses were in a little dip, the ground round about them was quite flat, and with his knees well flexed, Ally didn't jerk the camera too much when running. He carried on until the film had run out, and then rewound the tape on the camera. 'I can look through the viewer now and play it back to check that it has worked. I can't do it for long though because the battery will run out soon.'

Jimbo and Donna stood eagerly by him as he looked through the viewer going 'Ooh' and 'Ah'.

'Ya beauty!' he exclaimed. 'It has worked a treat.'

'Let me see,' urged Jimbo.

Both Jimbo and Donna got a quick look before the camera signalled that the battery had run out.

'That's it then,' said Ally.

With nothing to concentrate on, he began to get edgy again. Clutching the camera, he began to strut about and shrink back in fright at every little sound he heard. His imagination was running wild. All he could think of was Bruiser's face bearing down on him as he lay helpless on the ground. He could almost hear his strangled shouts for help which were being drowned out by the grunts and growls coming from Bruiser and his heavies. Ally was in a cold sweat. His stomach felt tight – he almost wanted to cry. Finally he could stand it no longer. 'I'm off,' he told the others. 'You two can stay here if you like but I'm going.'

Jimbo made to argue, but Donna pulled him back.

'Okay,' she said. 'I'll let you know what happens later.'

'Don't mention my name unless you have to,' Ally almost begged.

'Just go,' Donna told him.

'What a coward,' said Jimbo as he watched Ally scamper off clutching the camera.

'He was scared, Jimbo,' reasoned Donna. 'What was the point in making him stay? Besides, at least we know that the film is safe.'

'Wish he'd taken these blasted binoculars with him,' complained Jimbo. 'They weigh a ton.'

'Hopefully, we'll get transport home,' said Donna.

'I wonder how Robbie's getting on,' mused Jimbo.


Robbie had decided to take the cross country route, which as the crow flew was much shorter than going by road. Plus there was always the chance once he got on to his father's land that someone out in the fields would give him a lift in their tractor.

Unfortunately no-one was about and as Robbie drew ever closer to the farm house, the heavy ground was taking its toll on his lungs and his legs.

Worse was to come. When he did reach the farm house, no-one was about. The door was locked and a note had been pinned to it telling him that they were all at the flower show in town. With the cold air rasping down his throat, Robbie circled the old house twice on the off chance that a window he could reach would be open. No such luck. The whole house was as safe as Fort Knox. There was nothing he could do but to head for the town and the police station.

He didn't have far to go, but the first half of the road was straight uphill. Robbie urged himself on, even though he felt his lungs would burst at any minute.

By the time he reached the police station, all he could mumble was 'help,' before collapsing in a heap in front of the sergeant. It was five full minutes before Robbie had recovered himself enough to tell the story and the sergeant radioed for a police car to come to the station and pick him up as soon as possible.

'They're all doing speed traps, since it's such a nice day,' said the sergeant.

Robbie smiled to himself. Often before he had heard his father complaining that you never saw a speed trap when the weather was bad and conditions were at their most dangerous. He kept quiet and enjoyed the few minutes rest.

'I don't believe it!' exclaimed Jimbo, jumping up and

down. 'There's a crowd of hooligans with a tractor and bogey heading our way. It's hard to tell, but it looks like Bruiser's driving.'

'What are we going to do?' asked Donna, leaping to her feet and scattering the remainder of her crisps on the ground.

'They're heading straight for us. We'll have to make a run for it.'

'What about the rabbit?'

'Give me the bag,' urged Jimbo. Deftly he opened the bag wide and spread it over what was left of the rabbit. As he gripped the carcass with the plastic, the stewy feeling of it made him feel sick. Donna couldn't even look. Just the thought of what he was doing made her gag.

'Hurry Jimbo,' she urged. 'They're getting close.'

'Got it,' said Jimbo triumphantly. 'Do you think you could carry it? It's quite safe – I made sure that there was no goo that you could touch. Just grip it tight below the handle holes. It could be lethal otherwise.'

'Do I have to?' she asked tentatively.

'Well it's that or these huge binoculars,' he replied.

She took the bag from him and turned round to see the tractor only metres away.

'Let's go!' cried Jimbo.

They scampered off in any direction with no idea where they were headed for. The tractor pursued them. At least the hooligans didn't seem to have noticed the buzzard.

'They'll catch us,' gasped Donna. 'The tractor can go faster than we can run.'

44

'We'll have to go somewhere that the tractor can't. How about across the river?'

'No way!' squealed Donna. 'We've no idea how deep it is, and anyway some of the poison in this rabbit might escape into the water.'

'I've got a better idea anyway,' puffed Jimbo. 'We'll go through the forestry – they can't follow us in there with the tractor.'

'With any luck we might meet someone,' gasped Donna.

'Come on then,' urged Jimbo, 'we'll cut back and climb this hill. It's the quickest way. Why didn't I make Ally take these binoculars with him,' he groaned.

Donna, who was carrying the small binoculars and the rabbit sped ahead of Jimbo as they vied for the top of the hill and the relative safety of the trees. She had her head down and was just concentrating on pumping her legs as fast as she could. Somewhere amidst the noise of her feet thumping against the muddy ground she heard a roar and she looked back to see Jimbo rolling along the ground in agony. He must have fallen and twisted his ankle. The thugs were almost up to him. She started to run back.

'Keep going,' he urged her. 'I'll be okay – just you keep going.'

Donna didn't know what to do. She stood still debating it until she heard one of the yobs yell, 'Just you stay right there sonny!'

Jimbo, still on the ground, pointed towards the trees and urged her to go.

'The evidence,' he whispered.

'Of course!' she shouted and flew back up the hill again towards the forestry.

Before she plunged into the trees and out of sight, she looked back to see Jimbo surrounded by big, menacing youths.

# 8

Surprised to find that none of the thugs seemed to be following her, Donna was able to keep to the footpath. She didn't fancy hacking her way through the middle of the trees, and anyhow, she felt much safer taking a well-trodden route.

She wondered what was happening to Jimbo. There were five or six thugs, she guessed, although she had never had time to count them. Between them they could do him a lot of damage. Why did these boys have to go around in gangs terrorising people? Donna thought back to Ally's fear of Bruiser finding out that he was involved. Ally was joining the Strollers because he was too afraid not to. It was a vicious circle – frightened boys who were afraid of gangs joined the gangs to be safe – walk the plank or join the crew. Donna wished that Ally had been with Jimbo now. He may have been able to talk them out of trouble since he was almost one of the 'boys'.

Pretty soon, Donna was bounding down the hill and into town. She charged into the police station, having no idea of what she was going to say. Therefore it all came out in a blurb. 'My friend Robbie may have telephoned about a bird and a rabbit on the Reid land. Well the bird . . . a buzzard . . . they are birds of prey, it ate the rabbit and it died because the rabbit was poisoned. Robbie, that is Robert Salter, he came to get help and now poor Jimbo is being battered by a crowd of yobbos who chased us in a tractor and bogey and made Jimbo fall and hurt his leg . . . and he's . . . he's got a huge pair of . . . binoculars that belong to . . . er . . . someone else . . .'

Realising that she had almost given Ally away, Donna paused long enough for the sergeant to get a word in.

'Let me get this straight young lady. You and Jimbo?'

'James Smith sir,' said Donna.

'Right, James Smith. You two were with young Salter when he found the buzzard which had been baited.'

'That's right sir, and we . . .'

'And presumably you stayed with the evidence while young Salter came to get help.'

'Yes, and then Jimbo . . .'

'Then some older youths came along with a tractor and bogey and chased you?'

'And Jimbo fell . . .'

'Smith fell and hurt his leg but you got away. And now you think these boys are . . .'

'Doing him in . . . sir.'

'What's in that bag, young lady?'

'The . . . the poisoned rabbit . . . sir.'

'Am I right in saying that you have been running around in public with something as lethal as that?'

'But they were . . . we were . . . I came straight here sir,' pleaded Donna, fighting back the tears.

With that, the station door opened and in hobbled Jimbo.

'Are you all right?' Donna squealed.

'They just wanted the binoculars – I had to give them to Bruiser. He said he would give them back to . . . you know who . . . later.'

Jimbo moved aside to let a policeman in. He was wearing rubber gloves and was carrying a bag which appeared to hold the buzzard. A very pale looking Robbie followed him in.

'Your parents are all on the way,' said the sergeant as he put on a pair of rubber gloves. 'They will be bringing each of you a complete change of clothing and you will have to remove the ones you have on and take a shower. Your old clothes will be checked for contamination.'

He took the plastic bag from Donna. 'You needn't look too worried,' he said a little more kindly. 'The type of poison used would, most probably, have killed you instantly.'

They all relaxed a little.

'But that doesn't make what you did any less foolhardy and dangerous.'

Donna and Robbie bowed their heads.

'But we were only trying to save the evidence,' reasoned Jimbo. 'It would have been just as dangerous to leave it where it was in case someone else touched it. We were just guarding it. We only took it away because these . . . boys were chasing us. We knew it was dangerous, thanks to Robbie, that's why we were careful.'

'And that is why you will have my commendation.

You were all very brave in a difficult situation. Whether your parents will view your actions in the same light, is, however, a different matter.'

Donna prepared herself for the worst. Not only had she walked through the woods alone, gone to the police without speaking to her mother first and probably ruined a perfectly good set of clothes – she had been running about carrying a poisoned rabbit in a plastic supermarket bag! Surely her mum would flip her lid.

As it happened, her mum sat quietly while the sergeant explained the story to all of the parents. When Donna went to shower and change, she helped her to get ready, still without a word. When the time came to leave the police station, she thanked the sergeant for all of his help, shook everyone's hand and then led Donna to the car. The drive home was still silent. By the time they went into the house, Donna was shaking in her shoes.

In desperation she looked up at her mum as much as to say, 'Let's get it over with then.' Her mum looked back at her, very seriously. Slowly Donna detected that the look on her face was changing. Donna was sure that her mum was going to cry. Tears welled up in Donna's own eyes as her mum's face continued to break from its stern rigidity.

Donna felt desperately guilty. Her mum had been through enough lately without Donna adding to her problems. She looked away in despair, but her mum clasped her hands on Donna's cheeks and made her look at her once more. She wasn't crying. She was smiling! Then she was laughing! Then she was hugging her daughter and swirling her round the room!

'I'm so proud of you Donna,' she squealed.

'Thanks mum,' gasped Donna, joyfully.

'Just one thing,' said her mum stroking her hair, 'I hope you never ever find another poisoned rabbit.'

'So do I Mum, so do I,' said Donna, hugging her tight.

# 9

The story of their adventure had spread through the town like wildfire and by Monday morning, every-one in the class was gathering round to congratulate them. Everyone that is except for Karen and Shanghita. Ally was pretty quiet too and Donna felt quite sorry for him. By taking the pictures he had played a part in the proceedings, but because of his fears he couldn't take all the compliments and congratulations with Jimbo, Robbie and herself.

Things were so hectic, in fact, that there had been no chance for them to discuss the project with each other before the meeting with Mrs McKay. Donna braced herself for trouble. There had been no time to sound Karen out on her ideas for the project. Now, the first time she was going to announce them to her, Mrs McKay would also be there. Karen was bound to accuse Donna of doing that on purpose. Donna shuddered to think what Karen would do to get her own back. Ally had asked Mrs McKay if they could have their meeting in the television room, because he had the buzzard video to show her. As they all trooped down to the room, Donna crossed her fingers and hoped for the best.

The video was brilliant. Ally's filming angles showed the full horror of the act. The buzzard was such a beautiful bird. It maintained its dignity even in death.

'It could have been a dog, an unwitting child, anything,' mused Robbie.

'What is happening now?' asked Shanghita.

'The bird and the rabbit have been sent to the Department of Agriculture and Fisheries to be tested,' said Robbie. 'Once it has been confirmed that poison was used, the culprit will be charged under the Wildlife and Countryside Act 1981.'

Ally swallowed loudly. He wondered what Bruiser's reaction would be to that.

'Do you want to use this piece in your project?' asked Mrs McKay.

Everyone nodded except Karen.

'I thought . . .' said Donna hesitantly.

'Yes?' asked Mrs McKay.

Karen threw Donna a threatening look. That was all that she needed to spur her on.

'I thought that if we used this piece and contrasted it with breathtaking shots of the beauty of the borders countryside, backing it up with only music and the occasional piece of verse . . . well I thought that it would make a big impact while keeping to the conservation theme . . . like they do in television adverts sometimes where they put the message over . . . but differently.'

'What?' asked Karen incredulously.

'I think what Donna is saying is that instead of adopting a "hard sell" attitude, the message could be conveyed to great effect by contrasting the beauties of the environment we live in with the cruelty that can still exist.'

'And what about my lead-free petrol idea?'

'It's hardly very visual is it?' remarked Robbie.

'So all of *my* research has been a waste of time then?' challenged Karen.

'What research?' asked Jimbo.

'Well . . . I've interviewed my dad and he said he would appear on our video *and* pay the school a fee.'

'I don't think that we want to turn this into an advertising feature for local business,' said Mrs McKay doubtfully.

'Too right,' agreed Jimbo. 'I think Donna's idea sounds great anyhow.'

Karen tutted loudly and sank back in her chair.

'Right then, where do you intend to go from here?' asked Mrs McKay.

'Shanghita and I can get together and discuss the music,' enthused Robbie, 'and we can consult Donna about the words.'

'What am I going to do?' asked Karen.

'Ally, you and Jimbo can think about more filming. Perhaps we can go out one afternoon and take some shots,' continued Robbie.

'What am I going to do?' demanded Karen.

'What *is* Karen going to do?' asked Ally.

'She could . . . she could . . . sharpen our pencils,' offered Robbie.

'Get lost!' shrieked Karen.

'Only joking . . . you can keep researching . . . famous beauty spots where we can film etcetera –

Donna may find their history useful when doing her script.'

'Great,' enthused Mrs McKay. 'Carry on then. You can let me know when you want to go out for location filming and I'll arrange the mini-bus for transport. Karen, your face is a bit spotty. Have you an allergy?'

'No Miss,' said Karen, rubbing her cheeks.

'Very well, we'll finish there. I'd hate for you all to miss "*Home and Away*",' said Mrs McKay, grinning. 'You should get some cream on these spots Karen.'

'I will,' Karen assured her sullenly. 'Thanks a bunch,' she rasped when Mrs McKay had left the room. 'Thanks for letting us know what your plans were.'

'I knew,' piped up Shanghita. 'Robbie told me at music class this morning.'

'And why didn't you tell *me*?' demanded Karen.

'Because you were busy with . . . that cream,' said Shanghita hesitantly.

'What cream is this Karen?' asked Jimbo. 'Trouble with facial hair is it?'

'Shut your ugly little gob,' retorted Karen.

'You *are* a bit spotty though,' remarked Ally.

'I'm okay, honestly,' said Karen. 'It's nothing that need concern any of you.'

'Acne,' said Jimbo knowingly.

'Well if it is, I'm the only one here who's mature enough to get it,' retorted Karen. 'We're off anyhow,' she said picking up her school-bag.

'Thought there was a funny smell in here,' said Jimbo, mischievously.

'You'll be laughing on the other side of your face once Bruiser Reid gets hold of you,' warned Karen. 'When he comes in for his juice to Shanghita's dad's shop tonight I simply *must* tell him who's responsible for getting his dad into trouble with the police.'

'I imagine he already knows,' chipped in Donna.

'Well, whatever he doesn't know, I'm sure I can spice up.'

'Make up you mean,' growled Jimbo. 'Just you try it.'

'Why, what'll you do?' asked Karen laughing. 'You couldn't fight your way out of a paper bag.'

'The way these spots are going Karen – you'll soon have to wear a paper bag on your head so you don't scare people off,' retorted Robbie.

With one last tut, Karen dragged Shanghita out of the door while the others held in their laughter until she was out of sight.

Ally didn't join in the laughter. What if Karen told Bruiser that *he* was involved in the bird incident?

# 10

I'm all spotty,
I'm feeling really grotty
And I think I'm going potty
And I want to scratch.

It may be fleas
Or a tropical disease
Or I've been stung by giant bees
And I want to scratch.

I've thought about my bed
But they're going very red
And I've got thirteen on my head
And I want to scratch.

It's getting very sore
And I can't stand it any more
So I'm rolling on the floor
Like I'm about to hatch . . .

Donna put down her pen and grinned. She couldn't wait to show it to the boys in the morning.

Still grinning she picked up a pile of books. 'I'm off to the Library mum,' she called.

'Okay,' she replied. 'I'll come along in a while to run you home.'

Usually Donna resented her mum insisting on

collecting her when it got near dark. But this time, since she wasn't too popular with some of the older boys, she didn't argue.

'Hi Ally,' said Shanghita over the top of her magazine.

'Hi,' said Ally hurriedly. 'Is Karen here?'

'She'll be out in a minute,' said Shanghita. 'Can I get you anything?'

'Em . . . a packet of sugar-free gum please,' he said, 'and a can of Irn Bru.'

'That's a bit silly isn't it?' Shanghita pointed out.

Ally looked at her, confused.

'Eating sugar free gum and then washing it down with a sugary drink.'

'Suppose so,' said Ally vaguely. 'Do you have any cold ones?'

'On the cold display over there,' said Shanghita, pointing him in the right direction. 'I was only joking Ally,' she assured him.

'About what?' he asked.

'The gum and the juice.'

'Oh that?' he giggled nervously.

'What's wrong Ally?' she asked. 'You seem very . . . on edge.'

'Oh . . . nothing. Just need to speak to Karen that's all.'

'What about?' asked an even spottier Karen returning from the back shop.

'Well . . . you know how you said to Jimbo that you'd tell Bruiser all about the buzzard and maybe make up more?'

'Yes?'

'Well . . . em . . . you won't mention me will you? . . . I mean all I did was take the pictures . . . I didn't go to the police or anything . . . I wasn't involved . . . really.'

'What's it worth?' snapped Karen.

'What . . . what do you mean?'

'I mean if I do you this little favour, what do I get in return?' she said smugly.

'My *New Kids on The Block* album?'

'Got it,' she snapped.

'The *Dirty Dancing* video?'

'Seen it,' she snapped.

'A hand with your history homework?'

'Done it,' she snapped.

'What then?' he asked shrugging his shoulders.

'I want *you* to help *us* get Donna *off* the project.'

'How?' he asked.

'I don't know yet, but I'll think of something,' she assured him.

'I don't know if I like *that* idea,' he mused.

'Well, you better had or else Bruiser Reid, who I am *very* friendly with, may not be your bosom buddy for much longer.'

'Okay,' he sighed. 'Let me know when you've decided what to do.'

'Gladly,' said Karen grinning widely.

'And until then not a word to Bruiser?' he checked.

'My lips are sealed,' she assured him.

'What do you think you'll do?' asked Shanghita when Ally had left the shop.

'Don't know yet,' said Karen. 'But until I do, at

least we know that the cow-bag has one less mate to rely on. Talk of the devil,' she said looking out of the window. 'Tweedvale's answer to orphan Annie taking her books to the library.'

'Obviously her mum can't afford to buy her one of her own,' said Shanghita following Karen to the window.

'Look at those socks,' cooed Karen. 'They must have been white once I suppose.'

'When they belonged to whoever gave them to charity,' added Shanghita.

'How often do you suppose she washes?' asked Karen.

'How often does it rain?' giggled Shanghita in reply.

'They probably save up the grease for the chip-pan,' said Karen.

'It looks like she washes her hair in the chip-pan,' joked Shanghita.

'She probably sleeps in it too,' retorted Karen.

'No, that's what she uses the bath for . . . she doesn't use it for anything else, that's for sure.'

'Shanghita!'

The voice from the back shop made them both jump.

'Come through here at once. Both of you!'

They went through to find Shanghita's brother, Joe, looking very angry.

'I cannot believe how nasty you were being there, talking about another girl like that.'

'Och, it was only Donna,' said Karen. 'Everybody hates her.'

'I am sure that is not true,' he said firmly, 'but in any case young girls should not speak about anyone like that. What has she done to you?'

'She's just a . . . a horrible pest,' said Karen.

'Shanghita,' said Joe, holding her shoulders, 'what has this girl done to you?'

'Nothing really . . . she just fell out with us . . . and she's not like us . . . her father has left home and she's poor. She can't afford to be friends with us.'

'The girl has problems, is less fortunate than you . . . and yet you make fun of her?' he asked, incredulously.

'Yes,' said Shanghita, meekly.

'You are a bigot, a disgrace to the family. Your treatment of this girl is no better than the treatment I received when we first settled here. You behave like a racist, Shanghita.'

'No, Joe,' urged Shanghita.

'Yes,' said Joe sternly. 'Go home Karen please. I wish to speak to Shanghita alone.'

'But . . . the High School boys haven't come in yet,' moaned Karen.

'You can see those . . . those hooligans another time and in another place. Now you will go and don't come back here. You are not welcome in the shop. And get these spots seen to. They look infectious.'

'It's a stupid shop anyway,' said Karen and she grabbed her anorak angrily and stomped out.

'You should not speak to my friend like that Joe,' said Shanghita.

'That girl is not your friend Shanghita. She is rude

and she teaches you false values. I cannot encourage you to be with her. She must not come back to work in this shop. I mean it.'

'But Joe, she *is* my friend. She doesn't treat me differently because I am Pakistani.'

'And this Donna, does she treat you differently?'

'No,' admitted Shanghita.

'Then why do you treat her as an outcast?'

'It *is* wrong,' conceded Shanghita.

'Then you must apologise to the girl tomorrow,' he instructed.

'Can't I just stop making fun of her?'

'Do you think your actions have hurt this girl's feelings?' he asked.

'I suppose they have, Joe.'

'Then an apology is required. Do you accept that?'

'Yes,' she agreed. 'I don't know if Karen will though and I don't want to fall out with her.'

'Karen has her conscience to live with,' Joe advised. 'You must make peace with your own. If she is any sort of friend she will accept that.'

Shanghita wished that she could be so sure.

# 11

Karen did not accompany Shanghita to school the next day. Her mother had decided that it was time she saw the doctor about her spots. Shanghita was therefore a little less apprehensive about apologising to Donna.

When she arrived in the classroom, Donna was already sitting at her desk and Shanghita slipped into the one behind her quietly. She supposed it had been quite brave of Donna to continue to sit in front of her and Karen in the class after the treatment she had received on the first day of term. Shanghita wasn't sure that she would have stuck it out had she been in Donna's shoes.

Taking a deep breath, she tapped Donna on the shoulder. Donna turned round slowly, not knowing whether or not this was another trick.

'I just wanted to say . . . I just wanted to say that I'm sorry Donna . . . for the way I've been treating you this term . . . I'm sorry, truly.'

Donna was stunned into silence. An apology, even from Shanghita, was the last thing she had expected.

'It's okay,' she finally muttered. 'Forget it.'

Both girls heaved a sigh of relief. Shanghita lowered her head and Donna turned round to face the front.

Donna's good day was made ten times better

with Mrs McKay's mid-morning announcement that Karen had the chicken-pox and would be off school for some time.

Ally was secretly relieved too. With Karen out of commission she was unlikely tell on him to Bruiser, and he wouldn't have to help her to get Donna off the project. Hopefully, by the time she came back to school it would all be forgotten. Even Shanghita wasn't too disappointed. She didn't fancy the idea of Karen finding out that she had apologised to Donna. Sparks were sure to fly. This way, she could be pleasant to Donna without too much aggravation – for the time being.

'So it was your brother who made you decide to speak to Donna?' asked Robbie as he and Shanghita took a break from composing music.

'He made me realise that I was treating Donna as an outcast. As an Asian living in this country, that is a bad mistake to make. Joe made me see that I was wrong.'

'Did he make any impression on Karen?'

'I doubt it,' said Shanghita smiling. 'Karen does not like to be told that she is wrong.'

'I'm glad you are speaking to Donna now,' said Robbie. 'She has enough problems at home without us adding to them needlessly.'

'It must be hard when your father leaves home,' mused Shanghita. 'I am lucky to have close parents, and I am lucky that Joe paved the way for me to be readily accepted into this community. It was not so easy for him.'

'In what way?' asked Robbie.

'We were the first real Asian settlers here. Joe was treated like a leper for a long time. It was not easy for him to grow up in these circumstances. I was born here. I have known children of my own age since I was a toddler. People had time to get used to me. It was not like that for Joe. He was always picked on.'

'Is that why he calls himself Joe?' asked Robbie.

'He was given that name by the children because they couldn't pronounce his real name. He still uses it because it is easier. He feels that he is more like one of them with that name. My parents found it hard but they have respected his decision.'

'What is his real name?' asked Robbie.

'As I said, you couldn't pronounce it.'

'I have never thought of you as different in any way Shanghita,' Robbie assured her.

'I am glad,' said Shanghita warmly. 'But it doesn't make me feel better about treating Donna as an outcast.'

'Everyone makes mistakes,' said Robbie. 'Everyone except Karen, that is.'

They both grinned.

'Let's get on with the project then,' enthused Robbie. 'I can't wait to see it finished.'

# 12

As the days passed, the project came on in leaps and bounds. With Karen still at home, the others spent a Friday afternoon out, taking film around the borders countryside. There was superb scenery in and around many of the borders towns. The views of Selkirk and Melrose were spectacular from the hill tops. The river Tweed was never more beautiful as it flowed regally through Kelso. St Mary's Loch, near Moffat mirrored the surrounding countryside as a glass, deep blue on the sunniest of days. The nearby Grey Mare's tail, cascading down between the rocks, contrasted sharply with the still of the loch.

The early summer sun brought everything to light. The grass was never greener, the birds never sang louder, the hills never stood out more prominently against the sky. Everything seemed bright, fresh and new. A heaven on earth. They filmed the serenity of the countryside in all its glory, a stark contrast to the slaughter of an innocent buzzard.

Robbie and Shanghita had produced a haunting melody which was to rise to a crescendo and explode in horror with the showing of the bird. There were to be several quiet spots in the sound-track where Donna's verse came into its own, celebrating the splendour of the countryside and then mourning the death of the buzzard. They all felt it. They could all imagine it. They wanted to fire up the emotions of the judging panel, in the same way that the idea had fuelled the imagination of every one of them.

The good news on the baiting incident was happily received by all of them. The rabbit had indeed been poisoned and Farmer Reid was charged under the Wildlife and Countryside Act 1981. He stood to be fined up to a maximum of two thousand pounds. The local paper reported the court proceedings well, condemning the actions of the farmer and congratulating 'The Green Gang' for their vigilance. They were to be honoured by the town at a later date.

Farmer Reid had fallen on hard times and he was desperate to save his crops. In doing this he had laid baited traps to catch the birds and other vermin which he blamed for damaging his crops and costing him money. Unfortunately, his actions were dangerous and illegal.

Bruiser and the Strollers were not impressed and plotted revenge. Ally, still in the clear, heard about this and warned the others. All they could do was hope that the threats were idle ones. As Robbie pointed out, Scottish Cup fever would soon take over and revenge would be forgotten as the Strollers prepared for Hampden Park.

'Don't you utter a mutter lad,' warned Jimbo's dad over breakfast. 'I've got the ticket and you are coming to Hampden with me!'

'But Da . . .'

'Don't Da me. It's about time you got your priorities right, became one of the lads.'

'But there's . . .'

'There's nothing more important than this game lad. We've waited a long time to have a go at this cup.'

'But it's . . .'

'It's decided lad. You're coming with me!'

Jimbo turned to his mum for support.

'Leave the lad be,' she told her husband. 'Why can't he play rugby if he wants to?'

'Rugby's not for us. We are working class. Football's our game. It's about time that this boy got his priorities right.'

'And what about all these hooligans that go to the football matches?' asked Jimbo's mum. 'I don't want him associating with these Castles?'

'Casuals Ma,' corrected Jimbo.

'There are no hooligans at football, woman. That's all press propaganda, trying to incite riots,' explained Jimbo's dad.

'It was on the television though, when these animals threw bananas at that black man. I've never heard of the like. Not in Scotland,' mused Jimbo's mum.

'But Ma, it's a crime even to be bald on the football field,' Jimbo pointed out.

'You see?' said his mum. 'Idiots all of them. You're not turning our boy into one of them. No way!' she insisted, stomping out.

Jimbo followed her quickly. With his mum on side he had a good chance of getting out of the football. She *always* found a way of getting what she wanted.

'Football's okay really Ma,' he whispered. 'I just prefer rugby, that's all.'

'I know Jimmy,' she replied smiling. 'I just like to get your Da going, that's all.'

As he got to the front door, the telephone rang. It was Donna in an awful state.

'Come over quickly Jimbo. I've called the police. You should see what these animals have done!'

# 13

Robbie was already there by the time Jimbo arrived, and Ally came puffing behind him a few seconds later. The sight that greeted them was sickening.

'It's the mother buzzard,' said Robbie quietly. 'Someone has shot it with an air-gun.'

'We found it lying on the doorstep this morning,' sobbed Donna.

'It makes me sick to think that someone in this town is capable of such an atrocity,' said Donna's mum, shivering.

'It was probably one of your pupils, Mrs Watson,' Jimbo pointed out.

Ally nodded his head in agreement.

'Here come the police now,' observed Jimbo. 'They shouldn't have any trouble locating the culprit. Not after what Ally told us.'

Ally shot him a frightened glance.

'You *have* to tell them, Ally,' urged Robbie.

'What's the problem?' asked Donna's mum, sensing the tension.

'The boys that did this . . . they don't know that Ally was ever involved with the buzzard incident,' explained Donna.

'He is supposed to be their mate . . . one of them,' added Jimbo.

'But surely you can't condone this sort of behaviour,' Donna's mum said to Ally. 'You can't be friends with boys like these.'

'It's not that easy,' said Ally. 'They'll batter me.' Now Ally was in a really tricky situation – Donna's mum *was* a teacher at the High School after all. He was stuck between the devil and the deep blue sea.

'Not if I have anything to do with it,' said the sergeant, coming up behind them. 'Now which boys are these?'

Reluctantly, Ally told him the story of Bruiser's threat of revenge for his father being fined. He was up against two symbols of authority now – he *had* to tell.

The policeman took some photographs. 'I'll have to call in the R.S.P.B. again I'm afraid,' he said, shaking his head. 'I'm sorry you had to see this,' he said to Donna's mum. 'Tweedvale Constabulary will not put up with this sick behaviour. The culprits will be severely dealt with.'

'It's the children's safety I'm worried about,' said Donna's mum.

'I will see to it that they come to no harm from this mob,' he assured her.

The policemen cleared everything away, and Robbie volunteered to clean the doorstep.

'He's a farmer's son,' said Jimbo, 'he should be good at that sort of thing.'

Robbie didn't find the task easy at all. The very idea of the fate of that poor buzzard made him feel like vomiting. If only they hadn't found the first bird, perhaps the mother would have lived on. He wished he could turn the clock back. But it was no use. What was done was done.

Then there was the rugby tournament. His father was insistent that Robbie should play. Robbie had tried everything to get out of it, but it had been no use. The tournament was on Saturday and his father would not budge. He seemed to be so sure that the warmer weather would be kinder to Robbie's asthma. He argued that Robbie always had less trouble with it in the summer-time and he refused to accept that the improvement was because Robbie didn't play rugby in the summer.

He didn't want to let his dad down. He *was* a pretty good flanker, and he liked to make his father proud. But the breathlessness and the wheezing were so frightening, that with every game that Robbie played the fear of an attack became stronger.

As he wrung out the wet cloth for the last time, his mind went back to the buzzard. 'I think we should go to their home and pay our last respects,' he said to the others.

'Like, hold a service?' asked Jimbo.

'Something like that,' agreed Robbie. 'Perhaps it would help us to feel better.'

'I wish something would,' said Donna, heavily, 'I feel so guilty. If it hadn't been for us, at least one of them would have been saved.'

'Do you think it's wise to go onto Bruiser's land?' asked Ally, uncertainly.

'I don't care about Bruiser anymore,' said Robbie. 'He couldn't make me feel any worse than I do now.'

'We can just stand near the fence,' said Jimbo.

'You could play the music that you and Shanghita have written,' suggested Donna. 'It would be appropriate.'

'Perhaps Shanghita should be in on this too,' added Robbie.

'I'll telephone her now,' said Donna.

Shanghita was keen to come. 'Karen's due back at school tomorrow, but I don't think she'd be interested in coming,' she told Donna.

They met Shanghita at the end of the road and then stopped in at Robbie's farm to collect his flute. The sad bunch then made their way to the buzzards' home. There was none of the usual joking between Donna and Jimbo. None of the usual bickering about sport between Ally and Robbie. They were quiet, each lost in their own thoughts, each trying to cope with their own feelings of guilt.

Once at the spot they looked around in the vain hope that a buzzard would fly by. Jimbo thought he heard a 'pee-ooo' at one point, but no-one else did. It must have been his imagination.

After a while, Robbie put his flute to his lips and began to play the haunting melody that he and Shanghita had created. Tears welled up in all of their eyes as they waited for the crescendo – their own salute to the buzzard. Once it came, Robbie returned to the original melody, this time more soft and subdued, and Donna stepped forward. 'High on the wing, at home with the land, flies the buzzard through nature, each hand in hand. With each puff of the wind and each glint of the sun, fly the buzzard, and nature, together as one . . .'

They all smiled watery smiles at each other.

Suddenly, a car screeched up behind them. It was Bruiser's dad. 'You lot trespassing again?' he asked, getting out of the car.

Shanghita shivered. He *was* a big man.

'We were just saying goodbye . . . to a friend,' mumbled Robbie.

'I'm sorry about the birdie,' he said coming over to them. 'What I did was wrong and I've paid my dues. I shouldn't have used poisoned bait, but these damned vermin were ruining my crops. I do have a living to make . . . but I shouldn't have broken the law. I'm sorry for that.'

'It wasn't *that* buzzard we were mourning,' said Robbie flatly. 'It was the one that was left on Donna's doorstep this morning, shot by an air-gun.'

'Do you know who was responsible for this?' the farmer urged.

'We've got a good idea,' mumbled Donna.

'Do you think my son was involved?' he asked.

They were afraid to answer.

'Do you?' he asked, impatiently.

'Well, we heard that he was seeking revenge because we found the bait,' said Robbie quietly.

'An air-gun, you say,' said the farmer rubbing his big chin.

'Look. We can't prove anything, Mr Reid. We can't accuse Bruiser . . . er your son. We're just telling you what we heard.'

'I understand, kids. I'll be only too happy if I find out that my boy had nothing to do with this. But never fear, do you hear? I'll get the truth out of him. You can be sure of that. He won't be threatening you again either way. Now you carry on here. I'm sorry I disturbed you.' With that he jumped into the car and sped off.

'I wouldn't like to be in Bruiser's shoes when that man gets a hold of him,' said Jimbo, smiling wryly.

'Where did you find the other buzzard?' asked Shanghita.

'Let's go over and look,' said Jimbo. 'It should be okay. Mr Reid seemed quite nice really.'

'It was just over there,' pointed Robbie as he climbed the fence.

'No it wasn't, it was over there,' said Jimbo, pointing in another direction.

'I think it was nearer these trees,' argued Donna.

'But you were going over there to look at the sheep when you found it,' Ally pointed out to her.

'What memories you all have,' marvelled Shanghita, mockingly.

'Oops,' said Donna, giggling. 'I nearly tripped over something again. 'Wow, come here boys . . . it's a baby bird! A chick!'

'I wonder if it's a buzzard?' asked Ally.

'There's only one way to find out,' said Robbie excitedly. 'We'll have to take it home.'

'Will we be allowed?' asked Donna.

'It's far too young to fend for itself,' said Robbie. 'It's all alone, no mother in sight. What choice have we got?'

'Do you know how to look after it?' asked Shanghita.

'We won't be allowed to do that,' said Robbie.

'Why not?' moaned Ally.

'The R.S.P.B. will probably want an expert to do that.'

'I suppose that's only fair,' reasoned Shanghita. 'We don't know what it needs.'

'But Robbie knows lots about birds,' argued Jimbo. 'I know a fair bit. I'd love to look after it, but I don't think we'll be allowed.' He picked the small bird up in his hands and nestled it inside his jacket. 'Maybe we can *save* a member of the family this time,' he said hopefully.

# 14

Just as Robbie had thought, it was against the law to keep a bird of prey without a licence. The vet took Robbie, the others and the bird to Mr Ward, who lived just outside Tweedvale. He was a Licensed Rehabilitation Keeper. He told them that they should not have taken the bird from the field straight away. The proper practice was to leave the bird where it was for at least two hours and then to return later to see if it was still on its own. For all they knew, its parents could just be off looking for food, or they could simply have been unwittingly frightened away by the children. But once Robbie explained the story of the fledgling buzzard's parents, Mr Ward congratulated them on doing a good job. 'You must show me the spot where you found the little fellow,' he told them, 'He may have some brothers or sisters. But first, we'd better take care of him.'

Mr Ward placed the fledgling in a small cardboard box lined with tissues, and covered him up. 'Until he has feathers, he must stay in here so that he is warm enough. I'll only open the box out to feed him.'

'Where do you keep the box?' asked Donna.

'The airing cupboard?' ventured Robbie.

'Clever lad,' said Mr Ward. 'You have obviously read about orphan birds.'

'Wildlife is my hobby,' Robbie told him. 'I'd like to be a licensed keeper one day.'

'Either that or a trumpet player,' added Jimbo, grinning.

Mr Ward then went into the kitchen and opened an egg box.

'What are these for?' asked Jimbo, as Mr Ward cracked two eggs.

'I thought you would be hungry after your exploits, lad,' said Mr Ward, smiling.

'I'm not keen on eggs,' admitted Jimbo.

'Could one of you fetch two worms out of the garden?' Mr Ward asked.

Jimbo looked horrified.

'He's going to feed the bird, bam-pot,' laughed Robbie.

'I'll get them,' volunteered Ally. 'Does anyone want to help?'

'No thanks,' muttered the girls, screwing their faces up.

'I will,' said Jimbo, relieved to get out of the kitchen.

'Now,' said Mr Ward as he beat the eggs together with some milk, 'if you look in that cupboard over there Donna, you'll find the biscuit barrel. Help yourselves, and bring me a plain one. This little chap is going to have a feast.'

By the time Jimbo and Ally appeared with the worms, the eggs were scrambled and Mr Ward had put them onto an old plate to cool. Donna and Shanghita turned away with disgust as he cut the worms up into small pieces and mixed them with some of the eggs and some crushed biscuit. Picking up a pair of blunt tweezers, Mr Ward made for the box and everyone crept behind him. He put the tweezers gently against the little bird's beak. 'I'm trying to make him gape,' he whispered Sure enough, after a little persuasion, the bird opened his beak wide and Mr Ward gently pushed some food well down his throat.

'What if he hadn't gaped?' asked Donna.

'Then I would have had to force him to open his beak and one of you would have given him the food. I don't like doing that but sometimes you have to force-feed them at first.'

'Yeuch,' said Shanghita.

'They soon learn to gape though,' Mr Ward assured her.

'How much will he eat?' asked Jimbo.

'Up to his own body weight,' Robbie told him.

'Where does he put it all? He'll explode!' exclaimed Jimbo, aghast.

'Not all at once bam-pot,' said Robbie, shaking his head.

'I was only joking,' said Jimbo, going red in the face.

'I'll feed him about once an hour during the day,' Mr Ward told them, 'and at night he'll be covered up and kept in the airing cupboard nice and cosy, as if his mother was brooding him.'

'I'm glad I'm not a bird,' mused Jimbo.

'Why?' asked Donna.

'I'd hate to have my mum sitting on top of me all night!'

They all giggled.

'Do you think, once he's a bit bigger, that we could film him?' asked Ally.

They explained their project to Mr Ward.

'I don't see why not, until he's released, that is. Then we should leave him to get on with his own life.'

'It would make a fantastic ending to our film,' said Donna eagerly. 'Releasing a buzzard back into the wild. Our story will have gone full circle then.'

'Can we come back to see him?' asked Shanghita.

'Of course,' said Mr Ward, covering the box again. 'It'll be easier to see him, once I transfer him to a cage. He'll be stronger then, and a good deal more active.'

'I can't wait to see him hopping about,' said Jimbo, excitedly.

'I can't wait to see him flying away,' said Robbie.

They all heartily agreed.

# 15

Karen was in a foul mood by Monday evening. Two or three times during the day she sensed that something was going on between Donna and Shanghita. They didn't actually speak to each other – not while she was there anyhow – but they had exchanged what Karen detected as 'knowing' looks throughout the day.

That wasn't her only problem. Ally had announced to them at lunch-time that Bruiser's dad had found out that he was responsible for shooting the other buzzard. He had been grounded for a month and had been warned not to associate with any of the Strollers once he was allowed out again. He was even going to miss out on the cup final on Saturday.

That news pleased the others immensely. It meant that Karen had lost her leverage with Ally. There would be no point in threatening to tell Bruiser about Ally's involvement now – apparently Bruiser was the laughing stock of the High School. Ally wouldn't help her to get Donna off the project now. Therefore, when Robbie announced to Mrs McKay that the project was almost finished, Karen could take no more. 'What do you mean it's almost finished? How can it be? I haven't done anything yet.'

'Well, we couldn't sit around and wait for your spots to go away, could we?' argued Robbie.

'But it's *not* fair – I am Top Girl and no-one has consulted me. Mrs McKay I must protest.'

'I'm sorry, Karen,' said Mrs McKay, 'but Robert was quite right – we had to get on with the project. There is a deadline to meet, after all.'

Karen folded her arms, stuck out her bottom lip and thumped back in her chair. 'Take my name off the project then. I don't want anything to do with it.'

'I'm afraid the names have already been entered Karen.'

'Typical,' she said huffily.

'And frankly, I don't understand your attitude,' continued Mrs McKay, 'you seem to have been against this project the whole way through. That's not the behaviour I would expect from the Top Girl.'

'They *kept* me out of it,' she complained.

'That isn't true,' said Robbie. 'You've been at every meeting we've had except one – and that's when you were off ill. Just because you weren't leader . . .'

'Nobody wanted that either,' she pointed out to Mrs McKay.

'This was a joint project Karen. If you wanted to be leader and were out-voted, that's no reason to lose interest. You've got to learn to co-operate with other people.'

'It's discrimination,' said Karen, shrugging her shoulders.

Shanghita had to shake her head at that.

'Even you've turned against me,' she complained

to Shanghita. 'You shouldn't discriminate – remember what Joe said?'

'Yes I do,' said Shanghita flatly.

'And she's speaking to Donna now,' chipped in Jimbo.

'I thought as much,' said Karen.

'Enough of this bickering,' said Mrs McKay. 'Now you're changing the end of the film I believe?'

'Yes,' said Donna. 'Instead of ending on a sad note, with the death of the buzzard, we're going to end on a hopeful note, with the release of the fledgling buzzard into the wild. Mr Ward says it should be released in about a month's time – so we should just meet the deadline for entries. In the meantime, we have to record the backing tape, with the music and verse and then just slot the last video sequence in.'

'Can we do the backing tape this week sometime?' asked Robbie.

'That's fine by me,' said Mrs McKay. 'I'll organise an afternoon in the music room.'

Karen and Shanghita had walked most of the way home in silence before Karen blurted out, 'Well, I'm not going to speak to her!'

'That's up to you,' replied Shanghita, 'but I am. Donna has done nothing to hurt me.'

'Except poison you against me,' said Karen, ruefully.

'She has nothing of the sort,' Shanghita assured her.

'I bet she has, cow-bag.'

'We've had better things to do than to talk about you, you know,' said Shanghita.

'Like getting the project finished so that I can't help.'

'If anyone kept you out of the project it was yourself,' Shanghita told her. 'You tried to ruin it right from the start.'

'I didn't,' said Karen. 'I just thought it was a rotten idea and I still do. If my name has to be included I'll make sure that everyone knows that I wasn't involved.'

'Suit yourself,' said Shanghita.

'I will,' retorted Karen.

'Right,' said Shanghita.

'Right,' agreed Karen.

'Are you playing rugby on Saturday or what Jimbo?' asked Robbie.

'It's looking good,' said Jimbo cheerily. 'Mum's on my side now and she's making Dad's life a misery. We had haggis last night – he hates haggis, it always gives him indigestion. She hasn't tidied up at all. He can't find anything. He had no socks for work this morning – he had to go with odd ones on – one blue and one black. She's invited my Gran to tea tonight, but he doesn't know yet.'

'Don't they get on?' asked Robbie.

'They fight like cat and dog,' giggled Jimbo. 'She hates his drinking and his football and his gambling. She's a holy-willy, you see. She'll go on and on about him leading me astray until he's in an awful mood, and then Mum will threaten to have her back for tea on Wednesday unless he lets me play rugby. That should do it I think.'

'Poor man,' mused Robbie.

'How about you?' asked Jimbo.

'I'm having one last go at Dad tonight,' he told Jimbo. 'If he still insists, then I'll have to play.'

'You'll enjoy it,' encouraged Jimbo. 'We'll have a great team, no-one will beat us.'

'I suppose so,' agreed Robbie. 'Sevens is such hard work though. There is so much ground to cover.'

'We'll help you all we can,' Jimbo assured him.

'Thanks,' said Robbie. 'Perhaps I can get out of too much running if the other boys cover for me.'

'Of course we will. You just tackle like mad and we'll run up and down the pitch. It'll be a dawdle – just you wait.'

# 16

'Dad's been on the phone,' said Donna's mum as soon as '*Home and Away*' was finished.

'What for?' asked Donna.

'He wants to take you to London for the weekend.'

'When?'

'Friday night.'

'This Friday?' complained Donna. 'Does it have to be this Friday?'

'He must have a free weekend,' said her mum.

'Well, I'm not going,' said Donna flatly.

'Whyever not?'

'Because the boys have a rugby tournament on Saturday and I want to watch.'

'But I told your dad that you would go.'

'Why?' asked Donna.

'Because I thought you would want to,' replied her Mum.

'Well I don't want to . . . not this weekend anyway.'

'But it would be good for you to see him,' argued her mum.

'Tell him to come here then,' said Donna. 'I don't need to go to London to see him.'

'I suppose not. I guess he just wanted to give you a treat.'

'I would rather see him here,' said Donna.

'Okay, he's calling back later. We'll see what he says.'

'Looking forward to the rugby on Saturday son?' asked Robbie's dad.

'Well . . .'

'Your Uncle Jack and Uncle Fraser are coming along to sign autographs. They can't wait to see you play.'

'But . . .'

'I've told them all about you. You'll follow in their footsteps one day.'

'No I . . .'

'Don't be modest Robbie. You handle the ball better than Joe did at your age. You're a touch slower perhaps, but plenty of hard training will put that right.'

'Yes but . . .'

'And you've got a bit of puppy fat, but we'll get you working on the farm this summer. You'll be solid muscle by next season.'

'If I play . . .'

'Of course you'll play. High School means more work, but there's plenty of time for pleasure too Robbie.'

'Rugby's not always . . .'

'There's always time for rugby at Tweedvale High School.'

Robbie's shoulders slumped. It was no use – he couldn't even get enough of a word in to give his dad a hint of how he felt. His dad was so keen for him to do well. Now his uncles were coming there was no way he could get out of it. All he could do was pray that Jimbo and the others could help him out. He was playing on Saturday and that was that.

'Are you looking forward to it son?' his dad asked him.

'Yes Dad,' came the meek reply.

'Your dad wants to talk to you,' said Donna's mum, giving her the telephone.

'Hello Donna,' he said to her. 'What's this I hear about you knocking back the trip of a lifetime?'

'I want to stay here this weekend Dad, that's all.'

'But I've got special tickets for the F.A. Cup final at Wembley. It'll be great. Then we can meet the players afterwards. Your friends will be green with envy.'

'My friends are playing rugby on Saturday. I'd much rather watch that,' Donna told him. 'Why don't you just come here? It'll be great.'

'I can't,' said her dad.

'Why not?' asked Donna.

'Because I've *got* to be at the cup final. I'm covering it. I'm working.'

Donna was silent for a moment. She couldn't believe it. He was always working. If she wanted to see him she just had to fit into his schedule.

Her dad broke the silence. 'It's just as well I didn't go to any bother to get this ticket,' he said. 'Since it seems that you wouldn't have come anyway.'

'Dad, I don't want to see you in London or

Edinburgh or even Timbuktu. I want to see you here, at my home. *This* is where I belong. *This* is where I want to see my dad. If *you* can't make time for that then I don't want to see you at all!' She crashed the telephone down and ran upstairs to her room.

Donna's mum left her alone. She couldn't force her ex-husband to do the right thing by his daughter. She could only hope that one day, he would come to his senses and visit her at home. After all, not so long ago it had been his home too.

# 17

Saturday was a lovely sunny early summer's day and the park was smattered with families who had come to watch the youngsters play rugby.

Donna licked on an ice cream as she made her way towards the pitch with her mum and Shanghita.

'It's a pity that Karen decided not to come,' said Donna's mum. 'It's such a lovely day, and exciting too. I'm looking forward to the action already.'

'Has she gone shopping?' Donna asked Shanghita, tentatively.

'I don't know,' admitted Shanghita. 'She just said that she had better things to do.'

The park was aglow with colour. People sported shorts and T-shirts of every colour imaginable. They were almost like extras on the set of an Australian soap opera. The sun was so hot that it could have been Australia.

The park was adjacent to the River Tweed which flowed gently through the town that day. It hardly seemed any time at all since the river had burst its banks with the heavy March rain. Now it meandered sedately by, inviting some of the braver people to have a paddle in the still cool water. There would be time enough for paddling in the summer holidays, Donna decided. Then the water would be at a more tolerable temperature.

Teams from all over the borders, and some from Edinburgh were here to compete. As they strolled towards the pitch, the girls could see lots of huddled groups of players in their team shirts talking last minute tactics.

'I hope the boys do well,' said Donna, clasping her hands together in mock prayer. 'Let's see if we can find them to wish them luck.'

A few men surrounded the Tweedvale team. Robbie introduced two of them to Donna and Shanghita as his uncles Fraser and Jack, who had played for Scotland and the British Lions. They happily autographed Donna's programme for her. She secretly hoped that she could show them to her dad one day. She could not have met any sportsmen more famous than Robbie's uncles at Wembley.

Jimbo was so keyed up and excited that his voice was much higher pitched. 'I can't wait,' he squeaked. 'Just watch me Donna, I'll be up and down that pitch like a dose of salts.'

'He's like a boy possessed when he gets going,' giggled Robbie.

'He's always like a boy possessed,' said Donna.

'I've been on a strict haggis and Irn Bru diet all week,' Jimbo told them.

'Your dad didn't give in on Monday night then,' said Robbie.

'It took five haggis dinners and two and a half grans before he succumbed,' squeaked Jimbo.

'Two and a half grans?' asked Shanghita, bemused.

'I'll explain later,' Robbie assured her.

'Are you okay?' Donna whispered to him.

Robbie nodded his head.

'Okay boys,' boomed Robbie's dad. 'Enough of this idle chatter, let's get at them!'

Jimbo shrieked and jumped for joy. Robbie grinned cagily and trotted off behind his team-mates as they took the field.

'Just watch my boy,' Robbie's dad told the onlookers. 'Just watch him play. Poetry in motion.'

The Tweedvale team won their first match easily, but Robbie's dad took him aside after the match and told him to get into the game more.

The second round match was a little tougher, but Tweedvale ran away with it in the second half. With two rounds completed, Jimbo was the tournament's highest points scorer with five tries already to his name.

'And you're still not in the game enough,' said Robbie's dad. 'Let them see what you can do,' he said pointing at his uncles. 'You're a good tackler – but let them see the rest. Let's have a few dummies and tries. Run at them boy!'

Robbie took the flak quietly. He hadn't felt too bad so far, but towards the end of the last game, he had wheezed a bit. Quietly he took his inhaler out of his tracksuit pocket and disappeared to the changing rooms.

The quarter final was much harder and faster. The opposition boys seemed to be bigger and stronger than any of the ones they had played against thus far. At one point, after a hard tackle, Robbie had to pretend to be hurt to get his wind back. He willed himself not to panic, but it was harder to sit back, especially when the other side was bearing down on their goal line. The tie was level at six all, when a great interception left Robbie free with the ball and the whole of the pitch to cover. He had no option but to go for the try. He made it over the line to the roars of the crowd seconds before the final whistle went. The conversion attempt didn't matter. Tweedvale were into the semi-final.

At the touchline, Robbie's dad was delirious. His son had scored the try of the tournament so far. Therefore he couldn't believe it when Robbie asked if he could be substituted for the next game. 'I'm not going to change the team now,' he insisted.

'But the subs haven't had a game yet,' protested Robbie. 'It's not fair on them.'

'They'll get their chance another time,' said his father. 'And anyway, if anyone was to be substituted, it wouldn't be you. You're the class player of the team.'

Robbie was angry with his dad now. Even if he thought that Robbie was the best, there was no need for him to have said it when Jimbo was standing near them. His friend looked hurt and Robbie couldn't blame him. He took Jimbo aside. 'Don't listen to him,' he urged, 'he's biased. You're the player of the tournament with six tries already. Just you show him what you can do.'

The boys shook hands. Jimbo was certainly the star of the semi-finals. He ran the opposition ragged and added three more tries to his total. Robbie was not only pleased for his friend. It meant that he had less to do. They coasted the second half. They were in the final.

By this time Donna and Shanghita were almost hoarse. Donna's mum, who had been unable to watch the quarter final because it had been so close, had calmed down during the semi-final and had now recovered.

'I don't know if I can handle the final though,' she said, doubtfully.

Donna thought that Robbie looked a bit pale as the boys jogged back from the changing rooms. 'Are you okay?' she asked him.

'A bit sick – must be the excitement. We're in the final now. I have got to give it all I've got. My dad would love to see us win. I can't let him down now.'

'I'm sure he's very proud of you already,' said Donna's mum, smiling.

'Yeh,' agreed Robbie, 'but winning's better – and with my uncles both here . . .'

'Go for it!' exclaimed Donna, patting him on the back.

Robbie was in trouble almost as soon as the whistle sounded the start of the game. A crunching tackle left him badly winded. Under normal circumstances he would have begged to be taken off – but he just couldn't ask – not in the final. Before he was fully recovered, an excellent pass from one of his team-mates left him in the clear and he struggled towards the posts. To his relief, Jimbo raced up outside him and he was able to pass the ball to him before his legs gave in. He scored! Tweedvale were in the lead. Yet, all Robbie could hear was his father complaining that he should have gone himself. That was it. He had to score a try in this game. He had to.

The rest of the first half was a midfield battle, with neither team letting the other have a clear-cut chance. Robbie still felt sick, but his legs were not as wobbly as they had been after that tackle.

At the start of the second half disaster struck. Robbie fumbled the ball near his own goal-line and one of the opposition swept it up and scored. The teams were level again. Robbie threw himself whole-heartedly into the game. He was everywhere on the pitch. He tackled everyone with venom. He dived for the ball at every chance. He ran at the opposition, swerved, avoided tackles, sold dummies, did everything but score. With two minutes to go he was getting frantic. He could hear his dad and his uncles urging him on. His only thought was to score, nothing else was in his mind. If his body was telling him to slow down or stop he wasn't aware of it. Finally the pass he had waited for came. He was half-way up the pitch with only one man to beat. He wrong-footed his opponent to perfection and strove for the line.

He didn't make it. Everything went black and he slumped to the ground.

# 18

Robbie's next memory was of being fed oxygen through a mask as he was rushed towards an ambulance on a stretcher. He could hear the thud of footsteps behind as they sped on through the crowd. Patches of colour zoomed past his eyes. His heart was thumping. His breathing was strangled. He wanted to be sick. A baby cried, a dog barked, the thumping went on. The journey seemed endless.

Suddenly they were inside the ambulance and the noise stopped. There were urgent whispers. Someone held his head. Another his hand. The siren began to sound and Robbie wanted to cry. He gasped for air. He shut everything else out and tried to concentrate on breathing.

Jimbo, Donna and Shanghita sat pale-faced at the edge of the rugby pitch. Donna had been crying and now the sticky, salty tears were drying onto her cheeks.

They were stunned into silence. There was nothing to say. They felt empty, afraid and useless.

'Let's go to the house,' said Donna's mum, gently. 'We can telephone the hospital from there. There's no use our crowding the waiting room out.'

They followed her meekly towards the car. Their

legs felt heavy and weary. The milling people seemed to sense their hurt and made way for them automatically. Donna remembered Robbie's last words to her. 'I have to give it all I've got.' She prayed that he had enough left to give; enough left to get better. What else could she do?

'He's okay,' said Donna's mum replacing the telephone receiver.

They all jumped for joy.

'He had a severe asthma attack, and it's left him weak. But he's stabilised now and is resting. I've to check with his mum, but you may be allowed to see him tomorrow.'

'Thank goodness for that,' sighed Donna.

'We'll go and see the fledgling tomorrow so that we can report back to Robbie. I'm sure he'd like that better than a present,' said Jimbo.

'Perhaps Karen will come this time,' ventured Donna.

Shanghita smiled. 'I wouldn't count on it.'

'We're supposed to be helping the bird anyhow,' piped up Jimbo, 'not scaring it to death!'

# 19

When Donna shuffled into the bathroom the next morning, she was sure she could hear her mum talking to someone downstairs. For a Sunday morning, it was odd that anyone should have come to the door. There was no post, or milk delivered. They even had to go into town to buy the papers. She washed her hands and face and brushed her teeth quickly before putting on her dressing gown and bounding downstairs to investigate. To her astonishment she found her dad talking to her mum over a cup of coffee.

'What's this?' she asked.

'I came to apologise,' said her dad. 'It was wrong of me to expect you to drop everything and come off to London with me. From what your mum has told me, there was far more excitement here anyhow.'

Donna rushed over and hugged him. 'I'm sorry too,' she said softly, 'and yes, quite a lot happened yesterday.'

'Some of which we could have done without, I may add,' said her mum.

'So, I got a late plane home last night and then drove out this morning to see you.'

'How long can you stay?' asked Donna tentatively.

'For a while,' he said looking at her mum for approval. 'What have you got lined up for today?'

'Well, this morning, Jimbo, Ally, Shanghita and I are going to see how the fledgling buzzard is getting on. Mr Ward, a licensed handler, is looking after him because he is an orphan. Then, hopefully, we're going to hospital to see Robbie this afternoon.'

'Busy again eh?' he said sadly.

'But you can come too Dad,' said Donna, encouragingly.

'Perhaps I'll see the fledgling with you,' he said, 'then I'll have to go. But you must promise to spend some time with me in the summer.'

'Where?' asked Donna.

'Well, it isn't really possible for me to come home for any length of time, your mum and I . . .'

'I know,' admitted Donna, 'it must be hard for both of you. I'll go somewhere with you if you like . . . as long as Mum doesn't mind.' She looked to her mum for approval.

'It's okay with me, as long as it's somewhere sensible,' she said smiling.

'Right then,' said her dad, 'do you think you could spare her for a fortnight?' he asked.

'I could try,' she replied.

'How does Wimbledon grab you then?'

'Where the Wombles come from? Where they play tennis?' asked Donna excitedly.

'Not only where they play tennis,' said her dad grinning, 'but *when* they play tennis too – for the whole tournament. I am covering it, but all that means is that we have to watch lots of . . . tennis. And eat lots of . . . strawberries. And meet lots of . . . celebrities.'

'Wow!' exclaimed Donna. 'I wish you could come too Mum,' she said biting her lip.

'I've been there,' her mum assured her, 'before you were born. It's great! And now it's your turn to enjoy it.'

'I will,' enthused Donna. 'Thanks Mum . . . thanks Dad. I'd better get dressed now. We've to meet the others in half an hour!'

Robbie was pale and he looked tired, but a huge grin spread across his face when the others walked in.

'How do you feel?' asked Donna.

'Okay really, a lot better than yesterday. I just wish I'd made it over the line before collapsing. Then when the game was stopped we would have been ahead.'

'We were the best team anyway,' Jimbo told him. 'Every-one said that.'

'There was only one team better,' said Robbie seriously.

They all looked at him, confused.

'The ambulance team. They saved my life.'

Every-one nodded in agreement.

'Of course, there was one other good team yesterday,' piped up Ally.

'City!' exclaimed Robbie. 'I heard this morning that they won the cup.'

'Walked it,' grinned Ally. 'Strolled it, in fact.'

They all groaned.

'Your dad'll be pleased too,' Robbie said, turning to Jimbo.

'Yes and no,' replied Jimbo.

'He's not still going on about the rugby is he?' asked Robbie.

'No, no . . . he's not going on about much at all actually,' said Jimbo, mysteriously.

'What then?' urged Robbie.

'When City scored their first goal, the crowd went mad and my dad's mate threw his arms in the air. Unfortunately, the fist didn't just hit thin air . . . it hit my dad square on the chin and knocked him out cold.'

'He would be a bit quiet after that,' mused Shanghita.

Jimbo started laughing, 'Especially with a broken jaw,' he giggled.

They all burst out laughing. It took a stern look from the nurse to quiet them down.

'We went to see the fledgling today,' chuckled Donna, changing the subject. 'He's getting really strong now.'

'And he's got feathers . . . well some anyway,' added Ally.

'If the weather stays fine, Mr Ward is going to put him into a cage in a couple of days,' said Jimbo. 'He'll put some food in one pot, and some water in another, and encourage the bird to help itself.'

'He should be ready for release in a few weeks,' enthused Shanghita.

'I hope I'm okay by then,' mused Robbie.

'You won't be in here all that time will you?' asked Jimbo.

'They're going to do some tests,' explained Robbie. 'They think I might be allergic to . . . wait for it . . . grass!'

'Grass!' exclaimed Jimbo. 'A wildlife enthusiast allergic to grass! What a bam-pot.'

'That would explain why you get worse playing rugby,' said Donna.

'Yeh, 'cause his face is always in it,' laughed Jimbo.

'I might not be,' said Robbie, 'but they're going to look into it. If I was, perhaps Dad would feel a bit better. He feels really guilty and blames himself for everything. If it was something else, as well as the asthma, maybe he wouldn't feel so bad.'

'Oh by the way, Karen says she hopes you get better soon,' said Shanghita.

'What a lovely thought,' sneered Jimbo.

'I really think she meant it,' said Shanghita.

'Do you know what she's been doing?' said Ally. 'She's been telling everyone that she had nothing to do with the project.'

'Neither she did,' reasoned Jimbo.

'She won't be wanting her prize then,' added Robbie.

'That is up to her,' said Donna.

'Typical Karen,' mused Shanghita, 'cutting her nose off to spite her face.'

'That wouldn't help,' retorted Jimbo. 'She'd still scare off the judges!'

102

# 20

They all stood expectantly round the cage.

'Not yet,' said Mr Ward. 'We must give him time to get used to the surroundings.'

Everyone sighed and stood back a little.

'Let's just go a little further back. Let him see the space. Let him check the surroundings.'

'Let's go and jump in the Tweed,' suggested Jimbo. 'The suspense is killing me.'

'This could be a slow process,' warned Mr Ward. 'He might not even leave the cage this time.'

'Then what do we do?' asked Shanghita.

'Come back tomorrow, and the next day, and the next day until he does leave,' said Mr Ward.

'Thank goodness we're just behind your house,' said Ally.

'Luckily, this is an ideal habitat for the buzzard, plenty of trees and some open land nearby. I can see this spot from the house. That's why I picked it.'

'Will it fend for itself straight away?' asked Donna.

'I'll leave some food out, at the same times as I've fed it in captivity recently. I'll keep doing that until the food is untouched for a few days. Then I'll know that he is looking out for himself.'

'I couldn't do this job,' said Jimbo, shuffling about. 'I just don't have the patience.'

'I don't mind,' said Mr Ward. 'Sometimes nature needs a helping hand. I'm just glad to do it.'

'That's the essence of conservation, isn't it,' said Donna. 'You can't just take, take, take from nature. You've got to give something back too.'

Unnoticed by them all, a head popped round the side of the hedge. Karen too, waited impatiently for the release of the buzzard. Why was it taking so long? She jumped back behind the hedge again. She would never live it down if any of them saw her. She wasn't even sure herself why she had come to witness the event. It wasn't as if she gave two hoots for the buzzard, or a pee-ooo for any of her classmates. She was just sick of them gloating about what had happened and making up these amazing stories about what they had got up to. This time, when they exaggerated about the wonderful experience, she would know better because she would have seen it with her own eyes. Nothing very wonderful had happened so far. They were all just standing about, looking at a little cage in the distance, video camera at the ready. What a bore!

'Right then, who's going to do the honours?' asked Mr Ward.

They all turned towards Robbie, smiling.

'Can I?' he asked excitedly.

'No-one here deserves it more,' said Donna, happily.

Slowly, Robbie edged towards the cage. Ally approached it from a different angle with his camera pointed at the subject. The rest of them stood, crossing their fingers. Robbie took the top off the cage and then edged back again. The dark-eyed little bird hopped up on to the edge of the cage and sat for a while, as if preparing for the unknown. Ally stayed well back, using the zoom lens of his camera to pick out the bird.

Other than the dawn chorus, there was silence. Nature was still as it prepared to face a new day. Then suddenly the little bird jumped. One ... two ... three ... and it was off. Soaring above them in splendid animation. They all looked up, awe-struck. The buzzard was free and lived again near Tweedvale.

Karen watched from around the hedge, until she could follow the bird no more. It was a magical moment. Even she had to admit that. Ahead of her, the friends all laughed and shook hands. Their project was finished. They all felt better for the experience.

# 21

Donna didn't know what to expect as she made her way to High School on the first morning of the new term. She hadn't seen much of the others during the holidays. She had spent the first two weeks at Wimbledon with her father. It had been a wonderful experience. She had tea with Steffi Graff and had collected a mass of signed photographs. Boris Becker's was in a frame at the side of her bed.

Robbie had spent most of the summer at the seaside, trying to build up his strength for the High School. She had seen him once since he had returned. He was tanned and very fit looking. The new medicine he was taking seemed to have been doing the trick. He had spent many hours jogging along the beach and was talking about running marathons now.

Shanghita had been away too, visiting family and friends all over the country. She had so many cousins and other relatives in Britain – she would have had to have taken a year off to visit them all.

Ally and Jimbo had spent three weeks at an adventure camp in the Highlands. It seemed to have been right up Jimbo's street – all that shouting and running and thrashing about. Ally's dad had paid for them both to go. Apparently that had put the first smile on Jimbo's dad's face since he had broken his jaw, redundancy from work having swiftly followed his injury. Once they had returned though, Ally had got in tow with Bruiser and the Strollers again – Jimbo had hardly seen him since.

Karen had been no-where to be seen. In fact, the girl walking along the other side of the road was only faintly recognisable. She looked quite grown up, and a little sad. Karen's mother had been ill during the holidays. Even now her life was in the balance, waiting for someone to donate a kidney which matched hers. Karen must have had a difficult time.

As she crossed the road in front of Donna, their eyes met briefly. Donna was sure that she sensed something behind them, a slight hint of friendship. For a moment she was sure that Karen was going to speak, but then she turned and walked on, as if she had thought better of the idea. Donna didn't mind. Everything was going to be different at the High School. Pupils would be joining them from other towns in the area. There were new friends to be made, and of course, old friend-ships to be renewed. Donna couldn't wait until lunch-time so that she could look up Jimbo and Robbie. As it was, she didn't have to wait that long. She was summoned to see the head master half way through her first lesson. When she got to his room, her other five old classmates were already there.

'Come in, Donna isn't it? Your mother is an English teacher here. You are all present and correct then. Don't look so worried, my duty is a pleasant one.'

They all glanced at each other and shuffled around nervously.

'As you already know, at a civic reception in the Town Hall next week, three of you are to be honoured for the part you played in discovering and solving a crime concerning the baiting of a buzzard.'

Donna, Robbie and Jimbo nodded.

'Now Mrs McKay, your previous teacher at the primary school, has telephoned me with the good news that your project on conservation has won first prize in a national competition!'

The boys whooped with delight and they all shook hands. Only Karen was silent. She bit her lip and walked forward. 'Excuse me sir, but I . . .'

Donna also walked forward and stood beside her. She smiled at her and then turned to the head master. 'What Karen is trying to say is that she is as thrilled as all of us that our project has won first prize. It was a team effort, and we are all very proud.' She turned to Karen and shook her hand.

'Here here,' said Robbie, Ally and Shanghita.

'What? Where?' asked Jimbo, who hadn't been paying attention.

'Just nod your head, bam-pot,' groaned Donna.

Jimbo duly obliged.